I0626501

Jon Bragg Blue Essence

Kenney Myers

Published by Kenney Myers, 2021.

This is a work of fiction. Similarities to real people, places, or events are entirely coincidental.

JON BRAGG BLUE ESSENCE

First edition. January 30, 2021.

Copyright © 2021 Kenney Myers.

ISBN: 978-1736571118

Written by Kenney Myers.

Table of Contents

To my wife Jolene & our kids

Ashley, Kelsey, & Joseph.

May you dream as big as your support has allowed me to dream.

Sixteen

Jon

THERE IT IS—MY ALARM. I better get up, though I don't really want to because I can tell this is going to be another typical Iowa winter day. It's so cold in my room and, while it feels great under the covers, it is going to be wickedly bitter when I shed these blankets.

I look over at the window and, as expected, it is frosted over with a paper thin sheet of frost. At least it isn't ice, which means school will be on time. Yep, definitely need to get up.

Then it hits me. Today is my sixteenth birthday! I wonder what the day will hold. Will it be the beginning of an amazing whirlwind chapter in my life, or will it be a continuation of the current chapter that seems like the longest ever written?

Life in the small town of Grinwell, Iowa is nothing but predictable. Every day has the tendency to be the same, which is especially true in the winter when the skies are gray and cloudy for days and days on end.

I jump down from my loft bed and almost knock all my homework off the desk that is directly below. Then I end up stubbing my toe on the desk and realize this is about exactly how I expected the day would start off. A cold, painful start that has me hobbling around, looking for anything warm and clean to slide into before Mom yells at my sister, Jill, and me, giving us both our final warning for breakfast.

I have to take a quick seat and scan the room while I wait for the throbbing pain to stop. It doesn't take too long to survey my surroundings as, unlike lots of teens, my room isn't particularly decorated. The main focal point of the room is my bookcase that holds all my favorite books, which is near, if not past, capacity. It's a beautiful view, if you ask me.

See, I am quite the avid reader. I read as much as possible, which reminds me of why I'm tired, because I stayed up late writing in my poetry journal.

That probably sounds lame to most people, and I would never tell anyone at school, other than Marc who, as my best friend, is fully aware that I have a poetry journal, as I have shared many poems with him over the years. At the same time, I doubt a single person would be surprised. I am pretty much famous, or infamous, however you look at it, for being a book nerd. That's my own fault, though, because I carry a book around with me everywhere I go and take every opportunity possible to read, even if it is one page while I wait for a class to start.

I love books and the way they allow you to escape the present and explore new worlds. It's the cheapest form of travel, for sure, and doesn't require you to pack a thing, wait in any lines at the airport, or get lost as you try to find a landmark. You get transported straight to where you want to go and right where the action is every time.

Yep, I love books.

I'm not surprised I got off track there for a minute, as usual for when I think about my library. So, back to my poetry journal.

Last night, I wrote about what everyone in the school—actually, in town—is talking about. Our P.E. teacher, Mr. Keith, was out hunting when he was literally torn limb from limb by what the authorities think was a bear, but they never found the animal or saw any tracks. Apparently, he was out in the middle of the woods, hunting by himself, which is also unusual since he never hunted by himself. Now he is definitely gone in a mysterious way, which has never happened in our sleepy little town. At least, not that anyone I know can remember.

When something like this happens, I have a tough time processing it and am compelled to write a poem about how I feel or about the people involved. I store it away in my journal and unquestionably avoid posting it publicly. It's personal, and I wouldn't want anyone to think I was taking advantage of a tragedy like this to call attention to myself on social media.

I did have a lot of thoughts about Mr. Keith. They kept coming, so I was up late, finishing what was an extensive poem, at least by my standards. However, it was finally enough to clear my mind and allow me to sleep.

Anyway, back to getting ready.

Great! No shirts left in the drawer. I'm going to have to sniff the shirts laying around to see which is the least offensive to wear today. *Yikes*, not the one I wore yesterday. I don't need that grief. Then again, I'm not sure anyone really cares what I wear. Half the time, I feel like I'm the invisible man while walking the halls, totally unnoticed.

Ah, here we go! A school sweatshirt, which is always a safe bet. No one can possibly tell when or if you have worn one recently.

Stepping into my favorite blue jeans—dark blue, with no holes—reminds me about how I hate those fashion jeans with the fancy stitching on the pockets and faded *just right* to look like they are old but not too old. Yeah, those aren't for me. I like to wear solid dark blue jeans, that's all. I'm sure it won't earn a passing grade from the fashion police at school, but what else is new?

I better brush my teeth and at least run a comb through my hair. Not that I really care about how I look; I just want to avoid the inevitable conversation with Mom over the lack of any grooming effort. As if there is a ton to work with here.

I am fairly tall at five-foot-ten, yet I only weigh one hundred and thirty pounds. That means I am so thin that it might explain why nobody sees me walking around. I wear my brown hair high and tight, like I imagine it would be if I was in the military, but I am your basic, average-looking guy with hazel eyes who is easily forgettable but also comfortable to look at in passing.

And ... of course. Exactly what I wanted on my birthday—one gigantic pimple, right smackdab in the middle of my forehead! Wow, just ... wow. Whatever ...

I sigh.

"Jon, Jill, breakfast is ready!" Mom yells. "You have fifteen minutes before we have to leave, so step on it!"

Perfect. Here we go. I better grab a good book for today so I can hide my pimpled forehead behind it whenever possible.

I almost run right into Jill as she leaves her room, which is conveniently right across the hallway from mine. I mean, the builder couldn't offset these bedroom doors even a little? She is in her usual morning mood, giving me her death glare.

Jill is two years younger than me, but you wouldn't know it by the way she talks to me or treats me. She could probably pass for my twin, as we share similar facial features—hers obviously more feminine—which is a nice way to say we both have rather long noses with a bulbous tip. She has long brown hair that she frequently braids and has hanging down one side. She is a fan of overalls, or at least is right now for some reason. It must be the current style in her grade level. She is tall, lanky, and loves to dance, something she has done since she was in first or second grade. By now, I have lost track of the countless recitals we have gone to over the years.

"Good morning, Jill." Seeing as today is my birthday, I give it a shot.

She squawks, "Shut. Up."

Okay, maybe today isn't the day we are going to have an early morning enlightened conversation between two loving siblings.

4

New Town

Dustin

THE ALARM GOES OFF, blasting Whitesnake's "Here We Go Again." I cover my ears and moan.

What an awful way to wake up. What is this noise? Oh yeah, it's the only radio station that would come in last night in this Podunk town. Apparently, it plays 80's hits all day long. At this point, we can consider that confirmed.

Grinwell is about right, because this is a real joke of a town. Only, I'm not grinning, not even a little. And I do not look forward to being here long term. My only hope is we can find whoever, or whatever, we are looking for and get out of this place as quickly as humanly possible.

Ha! What a weird thing to think. Yeah, as quickly as possible; that's the goal.

I hop out of bed and ... Oh, it's cold, so cold. Is there no furnace in this crap hole we rented? It's freezing! I need clothes *now!* Warm clothes.

I can't get to the closet fast enough, quickly throwing on some black jeans, a black T-shirt, and grabbing the first hoodie I find. *Ah,* that's much better.

Oh man, I just realized this hoodie has the name of my old school on it and advertises my big win last year. It was pretty cool when the wrestling team gave it to me after I won the state championship, but it might be a bit pretentious.

I could change, but I really don't care. I earned it, and this sweatshirt is going to scream to everyone at this stupid school that I am a great wrestler.

Sighing, I can't help already missing my old school and friends.

Life was fine in Urbandale, which is basically in Des Moines. I mean, it's still Iowa, with long, cold winters, but we had everything we needed close by, unlike this little town that recently got its first Applebee's. Neat.

I scoff. Yeah right.

Coach and I—I mean, Dad and I—are looking to improve ourselves by finding someone truly "special." You see, my mother passed away a few years ago, meaning I got shipped off to my father, who I barely knew at the time because my parents divorced when I was still a toddler. He visited once or twice, but we were never close.

Our relationship got off to a rough start until he noticed my athletic abilities and, after testing them repeatedly, he pushed me to try wrestling. So, now I have been wrestling since sixth grade. But Coach took it to another level. He pushed me hard, harder than a dad normally would, which makes sense because wrestling is all he really knows. It's his life.

He wrestled in college, was an NCAA champion, went to the Olympics, and he never lets me forget it. He was actually surprised by how quickly I took to wrestling, saying that, in our family, this type of ability usually skips a generation or two, which seems random at best. So, since he says I have wrestling in my blood, he constantly puts me through drills to further my training. Plus, a fairly stringent diet, which sucks.

I have no idea why, but he is also a fanatic about genealogy. I think he spends almost as much time researching that as he does studying new wrestling techniques and training methods. He has traced our family tree back centuries. Evidently, we have other Olympic champions somewhere in our family line. I would tell you more, but frankly, I usually gloss over when he starts rambling on and on about that stuff. I mean, what difference does it make? The only thing that matters is how it impacts my ability to get to the next level and eventually get out of this town and this dictatorship of a family.

Anyway, all of that is the main reason why my room is full of trophies and medals that my OCD father made me unpack the day we arrived. That and I was held back a year when I was in grade school, so I have always had a slight advantage, being the oldest in my class. However, when I turned sixteen last year, it was like a switch was flipped on. I became stronger, faster, and better in every way, so I destroyed the competition. It skyrocketed Coach's career, as well.

Despite him getting offers from much-larger schools, even some colleges in every major city, Coach had his mind set on staying at the high school level and he knew we needed to stay in the area. However, there was nothing left for us to accomplish in Urbandale.

I have three more years of high school left and intend to get three more state championships, even if it has to come here in Grinwell, or wherever Coach might end up for each year of my eligibility.

We visited Grinwell a couple of weeks ago, as Coach is convinced our family tree has branches in this area. While here, we met the old wrestling coach, Mr. Keith. Coach wanted to ask him about their wrestling team to see if anyone seemed to be a "natural," and I tagged along, not having anything better to do.

Mr. Keith was a simple guy and a decent coach, but he didn't believe in the same type of skill assessment techniques that Coach does. He also clearly had no ability to protect himself. He ended up getting torn apart, literally, by a bear or some other animal. Honestly, bears are quite rare in Iowa, but I guess we will never know. It happened early in the morning and oddly while we were still in our little motel on the edge of town. I was glad to be heading out that day, and not because of the bear; I couldn't bear the boredom any longer.

Coach felt really bad for the school so, for reasons he never fully clarified, he decided to leave our other school in the hands of an assistant coach and to take over as head coach here.

The school was desperate to hire a replacement and get back to some level of normalcy, so here we are, and now Coach is the new wrestling task master at Grinwell High School, which means that I will be the wrestling star in yet another town.

In case you forgot, I *was* the state champion last year at Urbandale, which is fairly uncommon for a freshman, but not completely unheard of. I'm sure there won't be much competition here, in my weight class at least, but maybe there will be another "special" wrestler here. Coach clearly thinks that's the case.

Being the new kid isn't exactly new to me. Like always, I'm sure everyone will stare when I get to school, and I'll have to suffer through who knows how many introductions in every class? It's so annoying and a gigantic waste of time, since I am quite sure everyone already knows who I am. I *am* the state champion. That's something that spreads around a school quickly. And, of course, they will know I am the coach's son.

I'm sure Coach will have a plan for me today. I'm also sure it will not be pleasant.

It is almost zero six hundred hours, so it should be any minute now

...

Coach calls up the stairs, "Let's get a move on. We have a big day ahead of us."

And ... here we go, off to see what concoction he has ready for me to choke down this morning for "breakfast."

Grandpa is Coming

Jon

AS MY SISTER AND I head down the stairs, the smell hits. *Oh*, what's this? Mom has made her famous Belgian waffles? That's completely unusual, even when someone has a birthday in the house. In fact, we really only have those on Christmas or New Year's. *Hmm* ... And Mom is standing in the middle of the kitchen, wearing her work jeans and a flannel shirt. This day keeps getting more interesting, since she generally only wears clothes like that if we are doing a project around the house, like painting or organizing the garage. Her hair is pulled back into a ponytail, which is typical for the drive to school or a "work on the house" day, so that could mean anything.

Dad is still here and hasn't left for work yet. He is also in jeans and a thermal shirt, which is not acceptable work attire for an IT director.

Dad is pushing forty now, but he has managed to stay in pretty good shape, despite working a desk job all his life. He always wears his coke-bottle glasses, which constantly slide down his nose, probably from the weight of the lenses, and is decidedly who Jill and I inherited our noses from. Let's hope we don't also inherit his gray and receding hair.

Whoa! He hasn't even shaved today. Indeed, this is either the best birthday breakfast ever or they have something super serious to tell us.

As I ponder that, Dad clears his throat and, well, it looks like this mystery is about to be solved.

"So," Dad starts, "Mom and I want to talk to you about Grandpa. Since Grandma passed away, his condition has gotten even worse. He can't go back to living alone anymore—it's not safe—so he is coming to stay with us."

"We don't have any extra rooms, Dad," Jill argues.

"Yes, we are well aware of that, Jill," Dad continues. "If you just let me finish, kiddo, I'll get to that." He pauses then looks at me a bit apologetically. "Grandpa will be staying in Jon's room with him. You don't mind, do you, Jon?"

I quietly weigh my options when, in reality, we all know that I don't really have an option. If I say no, they are just going to make me do it, anyway. If I say yes, well, then that will make them happy and relieved to not have to force the issue. So, I say, "Not at all, Dad. We will make it work somehow."

"Thank you, son! Oh, and happy birthday."

Finally, somebody remembered. I was beginning to wonder.

Dad's statement is followed by a not so rousing version of "Happy Birthday," being sung by Mom and Dad, and mumbled by Jill.

Once the song ends, Mom says, "We also want you to be prepared for what has happened to Grandpa in the last few weeks. He has gotten much, much worse. Actually, he hasn't improved at all since they found him sitting in his favorite chair ..." Mom is having a really tough time getting the words out. After losing Grandma so suddenly, I'm sure this is even harder for her to process.

I should explain this is my mother's parents, but both my parents' families grew up here in Grinwell and have always known each other, so Dad is pretty close to them, as well, and for all practical purposes, they treat him almost the same as they do my mother. That said, Mom always plans all the family dinners and makes sure that Grandma and Grandpa have everything they need. She has always talked to them every day, at least for as long as I can remember. They are close. Well, they were close.

Grandma wasn't sick or anything like that. A neighbor heard some noise and went to check on both of them. They found Grandma on

JON BRAGG BLUE ESSENCE

the kitchen floor. The paramedics said she had a massive heart attack, and you could tell she was trying to work her way over to their phone but couldn't make it. They also said she didn't suffer for long. I suppose that's the only thing we can take some comfort in knowing.

Grandpa, on the other hand, was in the living room, sitting in a chair with a pile of old photos in his lap, staring straight forward and mumbling the same thing over and over again. Clearly, seeing Grandma pass away before his eyes put him into this state somehow. It's like he switched off and is completely closed off from the world. It's so strange, too, because, a few months ago, we all got together for a great Fourth of July celebration. They both seemed strong, fully had their wits, and Grandpa was joking around like he always seemed to do. He liked to pull quarters out of his ears and give them to us grandkids. That trick never got old. He clearly loved doing it and, well, we all liked getting the quarters.

"We are going to have to take him to different doctors to see if anyone can figure out what is going on with him," Mom continues. "It's possible he has Alzheimer's, though how it escalated so fast, no one knows, or some other degenerating disease. We just don't know. For now, Grandpa isn't really Grandpa. He isn't all there."

We are all somber for a minute, taking it all in and trying to be strong for Mom. We all know this is going to be hard on everyone, but especially Mom, who no doubt will bear the burden of most of the doctor visits, medication, and tending to everything else that Grandpa can no longer do for himself.

"I'm sure it will work out, Mom," I tell her then add, "No matter what he can tell us, I'm sure Grandpa knows we love him and we'll do everything we can to help."

Mom breaks down, and Dad rushes to her side to comfort her. A Belgian waffle slides off his plate and hits the floor in his haste to get there.

They are kind of over-the-top lovey-dovey sometimes, so I just look the other way and try to ignore it. However, Dad then makes Jill and me join in, and we stand there for a bit in a big group hug.

"If we can't find out what is wrong with Grandpa," Dad says, "in a few months, we will have to put him in a nursing home or some place that can fully meet his needs."

This causes Mom to start crying again, and we do everything we can to console her, as it seems like that is the most likely outcome of all this. Grandpa will probably never be the same. He will most likely end up needing constant care for the rest of his life, however long or short that may be.

I then realize that some of this responsibility is going to fall on me if he is staying in my room. "Is there some sort of training I am going to need? Will I know if he is in trouble?" I ask.

"When we pick him up from the hospital today, we will make sure we have all the instructions," Dad answers. "If it seems like it's going to be too much, we'll figure out another solution, possibly a live-in caregiver."

Okay, well, that's a bit of a relief. I'm happy to do whatever I can, but I also don't want to be the reason that Grandpa doesn't make it, or the reason he suffers any more than he may already be suffering.

Having managed to regain her composure, Mom glances at the clock then exclaims, "Oh, we are way behind schedule this morning. We need to finish up breakfast and get the two of you to school. We will talk about this more later. Your dad and I are going to do some work to prepare everything as quickly as possible for Grandpa. And thank you both for being so understanding."

"It's okay, Mom," I tell her. "We love you."

Jill nods as she shovels a quarter of her waffle into her mouth.

"We know, son," Dad says. "And we love both of you."

That's about as much of this as we can handle, so we throw our dishes in the dishwasher, grab our bags, our warmest winter coats, and then head to the car while sliding our leather gloves onto our about to be freezing hands. We will all have to figure out some way to concentrate on what we need to do. This will no doubt be a burden that we will carry for a while.

"Hurry up, or I won't be able to stop to pick up Marc." Mom says, cutting off my thoughts of Grandpa.

It's so cold outside that it's a miracle our van starts up, but thanks to the thin frost, a couple swipes of the windshield wipers and we are good to go. And, with that, we are off to school.

That is how my sixteenth birthday began, in all its glory. What could possibly come next?

Breakfast of Champions

Dustin

I KNOW I DON'T HAVE much time to get to the kitchen, so I take a quick glance in the mirror. Everything seems to be well enough in order.

I suspect I got my charmingly good looks from my mother, because Coach looks like a military drill sergeant. He is constantly on my case to cut my hair, which is the main reason why that's not going to happen. I started growing out my pitch black hair last year. Now it's about shoulder-length in the back but relatively short on top. Some would call it a mullet, but I dare them to do so to my face.

I will slick back the top of my hair real quick, and ... that is about all the time I have before Coach gives me my final warning.

"Locke, get down here now!"

Even at home, he never calls me by my first name, or *son*, or any term of endearment. It is literally always my last name. I don't really care, because that's what everyone at school and in wrestling calls me. That's just what I answer to now. I think I may actually try to go by Dustin at this school for something different, to see if it sticks.

With that, I kick it into high gear and make my way to the kitchen, which is so incredibly ugly I don't even know where to begin.

So, this kitchen is like a blast from the past and a far cry from the sleek, modern, all-white and stainless steel kitchen we had at our last house. This one has oak everything. I mean, *wow*! Whoever built this house had a serious thing for that one type of wood. The cabinets are oak, the center island has an oak base, the baseboards and floor are oak, and of course the table and chairs are all oak. I could describe more, but if you can imagine it, it's oak. It must hold in all the smells from the last thirty years, too, because this kitchen smells like I imagine a school cafeteria would smell like if they made every single meal and plopped it in the center of the room.

Coach has already created a shake of some sort that I am no doubt going to have to choke down. This one is so green you would think it was pure grass from the looks of it, and based upon past experience, this is not going to taste good at all. This usually means that he has taken every possible green vegetable from the grocery store and thrown it into the nutrient bullet, which is a form of a blender, and converted them into something that sort of resembles a shake. And it's super thick, which makes it even worse, since I can't down it. It's going to have to go down one chunk at a time.

In addition to this veggie delight, he has the usual laundry list of supplements for me to take, including creatine, branched chain amino acids, fish oil, and every vitamin known to man. I actually have no idea what is in everything, or why I need to take it. I just know my life is going to get really bad in a hurry if I refuse anything that Coach gives me.

I grab some water and down all the supplements as quickly as I can. *Gulp. Ugh*, quite the breakfast of champions. *Ha*, I guess it is.

The last thing I know is coming is something that he simply doesn't tell me anything at all about. He pours a tiny amount of a super blue drink. It kind of looks exactly like the bluest of blue water from deep within the ocean, but it tastes really good. After I drink this, I know I'm going to feel quite a jolt of energy. Whatever it is, it must be completely legal, because I have never been flagged for performance enhancing drugs (PEDs).

We only drink this once a week because, apparently, it is exceptionally rare and something that has been handed down for generations in our family. I snuck some to a friend of mine once, and

Coach got crazy mad. It was a complete overreaction, as usual. In the end, my friend said I was full of crap and all he wanted to do after drinking it was throw up. I guess maybe it is an acquired taste. I'm not totally sure.

I see Coach has been going over the family tree again and has decided it would be a good idea to spread it out all over the table this morning. This can only mean that we are going to have yet another conversation about my great-great-great-grandpa or uncle or somebody that I seriously don't care about ... at all.

Coach starts, "We are getting dangerously low on the blue essence drink that I know you love."

"And what does that have to do with our family tree?"

"Shut up when I'm talking!" Coach yells. He bows up and makes yet another significant gesture to show that he is the boss.

"Sorry, sir." I'm really not sorry. I don't want to deal with it this morning on top of everything else.

Coach continues, "We are hoping to find some of our family to see if they have any more of it."

I nod, figuring that makes sense. "So, are we looking for the recipe or some special ingredient that somehow only our family members have?"

"Yes, something like that."

Perfect. I'll take a side of double-talk with that heaping helping of getting yelled at to start the day, please.

"The easiest way for us to detect a relative is if they stand out in any of the following ways: They could be super strong, fast, smart, good-looking, or seem like nothing at all can really hurt them or faze them. We will start with the wrestling team and see if any of them can wrestle as well and as easily as you can."

"I highly doubt we will find someone *that* good," I immediately respond.

Coach growls, "Did I ask for your input?"

"Well, you asked me to look for someone with one of these skills, so yeah, you kind of asked for my input," I remind him.

"Very funny, Locke. Straighten up or you're gonna get a lot of extra work today in the gym."

"What else is new?" I mumble. "Sounds like a garden variety day to me."

With that, Coach collects all the documents strewn about the table and jams them back into his notebook, saying, "Just keep an eye out and let me know if you think any student in your class falls into one of these categories. I want you to start with this Bragg kid. Someone said he might have something special about him. Now, get your bag. I don't want to be running late on the first day."

I grab my bag and realize I probably should have just put gym clothes on, because there is no doubt in my mind that this day is going to start with me in the weight room ... yet again.

"You ready, Locke?" Coach bellows. "Let's go!"

I salute and respond, "Sir, yes, sir." I only do that because I know he hates it. And, well, at least I can make his life a little harder. He certainly made mine harder by moving us to this tiny town. It only seems fair he gets a little crap back in return.

I grab my black leather jacket and slide it on over my sweatshirt. Coach zips up his hooded sweatshirt since "real men don't need anything else to stay warm."

Jerk face.

Best Friends

Jon

MOM LOVES MINIVANS and has owned one for as long as I can remember. I mean, I get it; they are comfortable, and the doors sliding open are actually pretty convenient. We have gotten a lot of use out of this particular one and, with added expenses coming up due to Grandpa moving in, I'm pretty sure this will continue to be our primary transportation. That means, when I get my driver's license, which is hopefully soon, like possibly tomorrow, then I will be driving this when Mom isn't using it. I mean, it's a set of four wheels and gets us from point A to point B, so it will be fine.

I'm really looking forward to getting behind the wheel without a driver's ed teacher or nervous parent in the car with me, like Dad. That is going to be such a great feeling! I cannot wait to be able to go wherever I want, whenever I want.

As I dream about how much I am going to enjoy my upcoming independence, Mom pulls up to Marc's house. We have picked him up for school for as long as I can remember. Both his parents work long hours and are out of the house early in the morning, so we swing by to get him on our way every day.

Marc Miller has been my best friend since kindergarten. He is one of those guys who you just know will always be there for you. For what it's worth he has indeed always had my back. I mean, both of us are pretty slight in stature.

Marc is about five-six and weighs around one hundred and thirty pounds as well, soaking wet. He has a ridiculous mop of hair on top of his head that is full of curls. Whenever my dad talks about Marc, he refers to him as the kid with the big head. Dad is great, but he uses nicknames for everyone that matches their looks in his mind and almost never calls anyone by their real name. I'm not totally sure that he ever remembers anyone's real name. But Dad isn't the only one with a name for Marc.

Marc has a healthy passion for Norse gods and one in particular—Thor. For whatever reason, he has something on every day that has Thor's name on it, or a hammer, or anything that Marc thinks remotely resembles Thor. His backpack is probably really meant for someone in grade school—bright blue with a gigantic cartoon picture of Thor on it—even though Marc is a sophomore like me. Every year for Halloween, he even dresses up as Thor and shamelessly goes to school like that. This is particularly unusual because virtually nobody else in the entire school wears a costume. Frankly, I'm not even sure it complies with school policies. Of course, this means that literally everyone calls Marc *Thor*. He knows they are making fun of him—he is actually smart—but he doesn't care. He says he will take being called Thor over a multitude of other names that the kids at school might call him if they didn't call him Thor, which is a fair point.

As Marc comes out of his house to get into the minivan, it is clear that he most certainly has remembered my birthday, since he is carrying a ridiculous number of balloons, and it looks like every one of them has the name of a Norse god on them. He does this every year. I don't have the heart to burst his rubber bubble by telling him that I really don't want to be seen carrying around a bunch of balloons with the names of or, worse yet, pictures of various Norse gods on them.

As soon as he gets to the van, smiling as big as a human can, he says, "Happy birthday, bro!"

I tell him *thank you* and grab the balloons that he is trying to corral as he gets into the van before the door slides shut on him with all his overnight gear since he is spending the night at my house later.

19

Just then, Mom comes in for the save. "Oh, hi, Marc! Those balloons are incredible. I'll make sure to take them to our house so we have them for Jon's birthday dinner tonight. You are still coming over, right?"

"I sure am! Thank you, Miss Janet, that would be great! Unless Jon wants to take them to school today."

"Nah," I quickly jump in. "Let's save them for the end of the day so we have something to look forward to."

Marc shrugs, and I feel a wave of relief as I realize that at least one crisis today has been averted. I will have to remember to thank Mom for that later ... when Marc isn't around.

The next few minutes of the commute are predictable. Marc and I have a ton of classes together, so we typically swap notes and homework so we can look at each other's answers to see if we agree on them. When we don't agree, we typically have a somewhat heated debate over who is right and who is wrong. In general, though, we both have our core strengths. Mine are in English, Social Studies, and History. If there is anything related to Science or Math, we go with Marc's answers, because that is somehow how his brain works. He is a logical thinker, which, if you think about it, makes his fascination with Norse mythology even more surprising.

Today, everything looks pretty much the same on both our homework, so there is no need for a debate. Then the topic quickly turns to the latest news about the wrestling team as we drop Jill off at the middle school. Of course she doesn't even say goodbye.

"So," Marc says, "I heard a rumor that they found someone to replace Coach Keith already."

"Really?" I reply. "I'm surprised that happened so fast! I figured they would have a coach from another sport cover wrestling this year."

"Yeah, so did I. But, apparently, they got a really big name to come in and replace Mr. Keith."

I wonder why a big name coach would want to come to our town to coach our less-than-stellar wrestling team. I mean, who knows, right? People make decisions on where they are going in life for lots of different reasons. I am definitely looking forward to hearing more about this coach.

When we pull up to the drop-off spot, Marc and I jump out of the Sienna and wave to Mom, who shouts out for the whole school to hear, "Love you, Jon-boy. Happy birthday! I'll pick you two up tonight so we can have dinner together."

That's ... great, just great. Now I can look forward to people teasing me about this all day, no doubt about that!

Captain America

Dustin

WE PULL UP TO THE SCHOOL, which looks like every small school in Iowa. It's as far west from town as possible and backs right up into a bunch of farmland.

It's early in the morning and smackdab in the middle of winter, so there is light frost on the ground, which looks a bit like a light dusting of snow. In reality, it's wet, cold, and annoying, much like the way my day is starting out.

Coach already has a parking spot with his name on it. Well, it says *"Wrestling Coach,"* so I guess they put signs up by sport here. It doesn't really matter. I'm happy that it is relatively close to what appears to be the entrance to the gym.

There are a few other cars around already, but they appear to belong to students, as they are beaten-up pieces of junk, heavily rusted, and generally falling apart.

When we get out of the car, Coach wastes no time telling me, "Get into your workout clothes and hit the weight room. There's no time like the present to get started. I want you to work on leg exercises today, so squats, dead-lifts, leg presses, and whatever else they have in there. Heavy reps at ninety percent max. And make sure you find the biggest guy in there to work in with, okay?"

"Yeah, got it, Coach." I guess the ride cooled my jets, because I'm actually looking forward to pumping some iron.

When we enter the gym, Coach points the way to the boys' locker room then heads off in the opposite direction, presumably to whatever office the school has assigned to him.

Great, the locker room is lined with orange lockers with padlocks on all but three of them. I grab the closest one and throw my junk into it so I can get changed and on with my day. There are a few guys in here already. They take one look at me and just nod.

One of them walks over to shake my hand. This guy looks like Captain America and Barbie had a baby then pumped him full of steroids from the day he was born. He isn't massive, but he is definitely ripped. I take it this is the biggest jock on campus.

"Hey, welcome to GHS. You Coach Locke's kid?"

"Yeah," I reply. "You some sort of superhero or something?"

"Nah." He laughs. "The name is Brad. I'm on the football team."

"That computes," I mutter.

"You want to lift some weights this morning?"

"Yeah," I answer. "Coach has given me my orders for the morning."

Brad laughs again. "Yeah, I heard that about you. State champ last year, right?"

I nod and act like it is no big deal. But, as expected, my reputation precedes me.

I follow Brad and the guys with him over to the weight room and, as soon as we step in, I am pleasantly surprised. It isn't the worst gym I have ever seen. They have a fair amount of stations set up and a good supply of free weights. They are old-school cast iron weights, but they will get the job done.

"So, what did Coach Locke tell you to work on today?" Brad asks.

"Leg day."

He laughs. "Of course."

Nothing has to be said. He tells the other guys that they are on their own then starts collecting everything we need for squats. Then he grabs a bar and carries it over to the squat rack.

I decide this is a great time to find out a little bit about Captain America, so I say, "Looks like you have quite the group of followers here."

"Yeah, I'm the starting quarterback," Brad explains. "I took over last year as a freshman, and it stuck, so they all call me QB1, and that is my offensive line."

"I know what that's like—being a standout as a freshman. It has its perks, for sure."

I decide to test out this guy a little bit, and I have no doubt he's going to do the same with me.

We go heavy. I mean, really heavy. I am definitely going at max weights and doing more reps than normal. He is barely breaking a sweat with my max weight, and that says something about him. This guy is impressive. I think Coach is going to want to know a little bit more about him.

"So, have you lived here all your life, or are you a transplant, like me?" I decide to ask.

"Yep, all my life. It's a small town, but if you are a standout, that really works in your favor. I mean, everyone knows who you are, and you occasionally get some special treatment. I'm not gonna lie; I don't hate *that* at all."

"Like what?" I ask.

"You know, like free food, and you can walk straight into the movies and stuff like that."

I agree. "I think I could warm up to that."

He nods. "Yeah, no doubt you are going to see some of that love, as well, Champ."

I decide now is the time. "You can call me Dustin, cool?"

Brad nods again. "Sure, bro, whatever you want, *Champ*." He laughs, and then I proceed to punch him in the shoulder. I guess I now have something close to what resembles a friend in Captain America here.

JON BRAGG BLUE ESSENCE

We check the time and realize we need to finish up before school starts. I especially need to hurry because Coach is no doubt going to want a status update.

Speak of the devil ...

Coach walks in and calls me over to him.

I give Brad a quick fist bump then motion over in the direction of Coach and tell him I will catch up with him later. Then I jog over to Coach.

"So, what do you think?" he asks before I even reach him.

I catch my breath and report, "Yeah, his name is Brad, and he is the starting quarterback on the football team. He is ... pretty strong and seems like he could be a natural. Either that or he is pumped full of steroids or something."

Coach smiles. "Good work, Locke."

I'm a bit taken aback. That was almost a compliment.

"Thanks, Coach!"

A small, heavyset man walks in, and Coach flicks his wrist, sending me on my way to the showers before school starts.

Blue Eyes

Jon

IMMEDIATELY AFTER MOM pulls away, several people within earshot start mocking me.

"*Love you, Jon-boy. Happy birthday!*"

Yep, that's going to be fun to deal with *all* day. So, the points Mom won by averting the balloon travesty has been lost by her glorious send-off.

Look, I need to cut her some slack. I mean, at least she cares and isn't afraid to show it. I'm lucky to have a Mom like her, so I am going to decide to accept any crap people throw my way and remember how blessed I truly am. Well, that's my plan at least ... until I see *her*.

I get lost in her deep blue eyes every time ...

Jess Friggens, aka Friggie, is a walking advertisement for the perfect girl, and everyone in the entire school seems to feel the same way.

She has long, blonde hair, is super fit, and has skin that seems to always have the perfect tan. Unfortunately, she also has Brad Dillon, otherwise known an QB1, leeching on her at all times.

As she walks by, I take in the most amazing perfume ever. Honestly, I don't know if it is perfume or just how she smells, but I do know that it is amazing.

"Happy birthday, Jon," she tells me.

Oh no, she heard, as well!

Brad cannot resist mocking me. "*Love you, Jon-boy.*"

I don't know why, but sometimes words can be so incredibly annoying, depending upon who says them. When Brad says this, I want to punch him in the face so badly that I can barely stand it. Of course, that would be literally insane because he is QB1, and I am, at best, the resident book nerd. He would literally pummel me into the ground in, like, five seconds, and I would be even more embarrassed. So, I am stuck with the witty reply of, "Thanks, guys."

They laugh.

Marc snaps me out of it. "Dude, give up on that and ignore them. Jess is always going to be with someone like that, and we both know it."

I nod, because of course Marc is right. And honestly, I completely understand why that is the case. The most amazing girl in school should be with the most amazing guy, and judging by modern standards—essentially, any standards since the beginning of time—Brad is absolutely that guy. He is a tall, blonde hair, blue-eyed, set of walking six-pack abs. He has always been the most athletic and, to top it off, he has perfect grades, so I can't even take any comfort in him being a dumb jock.

We head through the doors when we hear the announcement for everyone to meet in the gym. That's rather unusual. It hasn't happened since they told us all about Mr. Keith.

Oh yeah, Marc said something about them having hired a replacement PE instructor and wrestling coach. This must be about that.

Like a herd of cattle being led to their demise, we all begin to make our way to the gym. It's quite amazing how disorganized a group of kids can be when they are trying, or mostly trying, to get some place. I'm sure some people are planning ways to skip this little pep talk that is no doubt about to go down.

We all pack into the bleachers and sit patiently, waiting for Mr. Douglas, the school principal, to stand up and deliver the message. There is a fairly large man beside him who is clearly the aforementioned new teacher and coach. He is significantly larger than Mr. Keith was, and the way he looks at everyone with those steely-gray eyes as we walk in makes it seem like he is staring into our souls, trying to tell whether we are worthy of his presence or not. The guy looks intense, to say the least.

As the last of the stragglers take their seats, Mr. Douglas begins to address us.

Mr. Douglas is no small man, either, but instead of being built like a brick wall, he's incredibly heavy with a belly that hangs significantly over his belt in a way that can only be described as uncomfortable looking. He is also completely bald and has a mustache that is super thick and consumes his entire upper lip, if he even has one. I guess we will never know.

"Good morning, everyone. With the loss of Coach Keith still weighing heavily upon us, we have at least a little bit of good news. We are fortunate to have Coach Locke join us from Urbandale as our new PE teacher and wrestling coach. Coach Locke is an accomplished wrestler, as a former NCAA champion and an Olympic gold medalist. We are incredibly lucky to have him here at Grinwell High. How about a hand for Coach Locke?"

Noting this is our cue, all of us begin clapping, but we are also sincerely impressed. It makes sense that this gigantic man before us is accomplished. He definitely carries himself that way and is intimidating in every sense of the word.

Coach Locke steps up to the microphone. "Thank you, Mr. Douglas, for that incredible introduction. It's an honor to be here, taking over for someone as well liked as Coach Keith. I will do my best to fill his shoes and make sure the wrestling team doesn't drop a beat."

One of the wrestlers from last year yells out from the crowd, "Go Tigers!" and then everyone lets out a fake roar, except Marc and me because, well, that's kind of stupid in our opinion.

Coach Locke continues, "My son, Dustin, and I are coming off a great year at Urbandale with Dustin winning the state championship.

We are looking forward to working with the team this year to see if more wrestlers can make it to the top of the Iowa wrestling mountain."

We give another round of applause, which seems to satisfy Coach Locke, as he backs away from the microphone.

Mr. Douglas steps back up. "We wanted to make sure to welcome Coach Locke and let all of you know that we are working hard to get back to normal PE classes and to make sure the wrestling team is in good hands. Have a great day. And now, please, head straight to your first period class and check in with your teachers!" With those words, the assembly is over and the stomping on the bleachers begins as people make as much noise as possible exiting the bleachers and the gym. It's really quite impressive how loud that can be, once again, for no apparent reason.

Marc and I look at each other and shrug, deciding to wait out the crowd before heading for our first period English class. No reason to follow along like sheep. *Baa!*

We Assemble

Dustin

EVERYONE HAD ALREADY left the locker room by the time I got done talking to Coach, which basically meant I had literally no time to get cleaned up and ready for class.

I scrounge around, trying to find a towel to use and making sure there is soap in the dispenser of at least one of the shower stalls—yes, I have been trapped by that one too many times.

The floor in the locker room shower has that kind of slick, gross feeling that can only be in a boys' locker room, and it smells like everyone got their gym socks wet and hung them up to dry. Other than that, I have what I need and plan to make this as quick as possible and be on my way.

As I am pulling my sweatshirt back on, I hear an announcement over the intercom. *"All students need to report to the gym for a special assembly."*

Great, I have a pretty good idea what *that* is all about. I'm sure they are going to introduce Coach Locke. All I can hope for is that they won't bring me into the conversation, especially in front of the entire school. It's already bad enough that I have to deal with being the new kid and whatever rumors are already circulating about me.

I hurry up then step out of the locker room so I can follow someone to wherever I'm supposed to go for this fun little meet and greet.

As I'm walking through the hallway, I hear someone shout out, "Champ, over here!"

I look up and of course it is Captain America, and he has quite the attractive girl on his arm. She is tall and skinny and clearly in good shape, with long, flowing blonde hair that looks as natural as the sun, and her eyes are so blue. I know I have seen that color somewhere before. They are attractive. I think I need to get to know this girl.

For that reason alone, I decide to walk over to where Captain America is and follow him all the way to the gym. I will sit with him and the entire football team for this assembly.

Once we finally make our way to our seats, the fat dude who came into the weight room for Coach earlier gets up and starts blubbering about how difficult the last couple of weeks have been, and then some other stuff that means nothing to me. Then he introduces Coach as the new PE teacher.

Coach then goes on and on about all of his accomplishments, including the fact that he is a great Olympic wrestler. If I only had a dime for every time I have heard someone refer to Coach as an Olympian, I would be rich enough to have my own car, at a minimum. That said, all of this seems harmless until Coach does what I was dreading. He actually mentions me in his little speech and calls me *Dustin* in front of everyone. *Ha, what a joke!* He doesn't even call me Dustin at home, let alone in public. I wonder what his angle is here. Regardless, I'm going to have to deal with people wanting to talk to me now. How lame.

The assembly finally ends, and we are dismissed to go to our first class of the day. Now I am back to dreading going to English, especially since I have no idea whatsoever which direction to go to get to the class.

Captain America comes to the rescue. The genius asks, "Don't know where to go?"

"No, I know where I am supposed to go, which is English. I just don't know where it is."

He thinks this is funny for some reason, but I'm not amused.

"Okay, Champ, go down the hallway"—he points straight in front of us—"turn right, and it's the third classroom on the left. Can you remember that?"

"Yeah, thanks. See you around."

Since the school is so small, I probably could have simply walked up and down each hall and still had time to ask someone for directions, but I have to admit, this is faster.

I walk into the classroom, and it is like a blast from the past. There are individual desks placed in six rows, five desks deep. It looks more like a grade school classroom than it does a high school class.

At my old school, most classrooms were more of an auditorium style, with comfortable seats. Really, the best way to describe them would be more like a small movie theater. That is glaringly not the case here. Here, we have your basic metal desk bottom with a particle board slab mounted on top for you to slide into and try to find some way to get remotely comfortable. I have an additional problem being I don't know exactly where I want to sit.

I see a couple of nerds walk in and can tell they are nerds for two reasons. The one in the lead is short, skinny, and hugging a book that he is clearly going to sit down and immediately read. The other one has a grade-school backpack on that is bright blue with a stupid picture of Thor on the side.

I see them moving in toward a seat and decide to have a little bit of fun with one of them.

As Thor moves closer, I hear a couple of guys even address him as Thor. *Ha, that's hilarious!* Well, at least I don't have to ask this guy's name. He is definitely the one I will pick on.

Just as Thor goes to grab a seat, I say, "Yo, Thor, that's gonna be *my* seat. You don't have a problem with that, do you?" And yes, that was delivered with my best imposing stare.

Thor takes a good look at me and is apparently a little frightened by what he sees, as he says, "No, sir, no problem at all." He then proceeds to walk to the back of the room and takes the only empty seat that is left in the class.

Yep, that guy is a loser, for sure.

Smooth Move

Jon

AS MARC IS PEOPLE-WATCHING while all the students exited the gym, I had already cracked open *Romeo and Juliet* and continued reading. I have read it before, but it's one of the books that is on the reading list for English class, and I want to be sure that it's fresh in my mind when we cover it this week.

Unfortunately, it didn't take long for the stampede to be reduced to silence, so I had to shut it down as Marc tapped me on the shoulder to let me know that the coast was clear and we needed to head to class.

I must have read a little longer than I thought because we had to run since the hallways were mostly cleared and all we could hear was a dull roar coming from each classroom we passed and the sound of our sneakers squeaking against the tile floor.

Then, when we walked into English, we passed who is clearly the new kid, standing off to the side, waiting to grab a seat. Since we're in the middle of the school year, we know everyone who is supposed to be in our class and already have a pretty clear seating arrangement. The seats aren't assigned, but we all sit in the same place, anyway, because that's what we do.

Mr. Young, another overweight teacher with bushy red hair and tiny round glasses, was scrawling an assignment on the chalkboard as Marc and I headed toward our usual seats in the front.

Then, as we were getting ready to sit, the new kid, sporting a weirdly out of the times mullet, walked over to us. We offered a quick wave, assuming he was going to pass on by and head to the back of the class, but that was obviously wishful thinking and not at all how my day has been going.

Instead, the new kid cleared his throat and said something like, *"Ahem. Thor, that looks like my seat. You don't mind, do you?"*

Now I look at Marc, recognizing that look in his eyes. He is not good with confrontation and is looking everywhere but directly at the new kid.

The new kid smiles and takes a seat, forcing either Marc or myself to take the walk of shame to the last seat in the back of the classroom passing all the other kids who are now watching the interaction. Marc makes the move first and, since there are no other options, I take my normal seat next to the new kid.

Evidently, this guy likes to stare at people, because he is looking at me like I have my zipper down. Wait a minute—do I have my zipper down? Nope. It's just him. *Whew.*

This continues until Mr. Young finishes writing on the chalkboard and turns around. He notices the new kid and asks, "Mr. Locke, I presume?"

The new kid nods.

"Class, I would like all of you to welcome Dustin Locke. He is Coach Locke's son and, to my understanding, quite the wrestler."

Nobody says anything, but everyone takes a good look at Dustin.

He stands really quickly and just raises his hand and nods at all of us. It's one of those half-stand, half-sit jobs, and you can tell he doesn't really care for this rousing introduction. This sort of makes me wonder if he is actually halfway normal. I don't think anyone would like to be introduced as a teacher's kid, especially after the pomp and circumstance we all just witnessed in the assembly.

We spend the rest of the class discussing the Montague and Capulet feud and how that might have started and why it is being perpetuated. Mr. Young expands on that by discussing other types of famous families who have feuded over the years. As usual, he seems to like to throw in what he considers "modern pop" culture by comparing this feud to various artists who are feuding on social media. This is where he starts to lose me. I don't have any interest in social media whatsoever, nor do I think this feud needs to be explained. I get it just fine as it was written.

I decide to read ahead as much as possible and give the occasional nod. I'm sure whatever question he might ask me will be easy enough to provide if he happens to call on me for some reason.

Every once in a while, I come out of the book to hear a word or two. Now he is talking about some sort of feud between Taylor Swift and Katy Perry. That's all I need to hear to go back into mute mode and keep reading.

Before I even know it, the bell rings and our shortened first period class is over. Everyone shuffles past as I sit a bit longer, engrossed in the page I am on.

Marc swings by and taps me on the shoulder. I know it's him without even looking up.

I gather what I can, leaving my thumb in the book, and as soon as we are outside the classroom, I quickly try to finish the page that I am on so I can end at a natural breaking point.

Since my head is down, of course I don't see that the new kid has stopped directly in front of me, and I walk straight into him with the book smashing me in the face. Before I realize completely what is happening, I immediately try to diffuse the situation.

"Sorry, sorry. I should have been watching where I was going. I didn't mean to run into you ..." I look up and quickly back down to add, "Dustin."

I already know this isn't going to be good, but then I turn to look away from him and see Jess and Brad standing with Dustin, which must be why he stopped in the middle of the hallway. Of course he is friends with Brad already. That makes total sense. It's like the best jocks have some sort of magnetic force that draws them together into a nice, little forceful unit.

Instead of Dustin letting me have it, it's Brad who laughs and lets out, "Smooth move, *Jon-boy*."

Great, I sincerely hope that nickname doesn't stick. It took me years to shake it off in grade school and junior high.

Marc tugs on my arm, and I lower my head and follow in the direction he is walking. That's twice I have been embarrassed in front of Jess today. That must be some kind of record.

Goulash

Dustin

EVERY CLASS BASICALLY starts the same way. I barely make it to the class on time to find that there are few seats, if any, available, so I stand and wait to figure out where I am going to cop a squat for the next hour while the teacher has their back to the students, doing whatever it is they do to try to prepare for the next period. Some of them appear to be building up the courage to face another wall of blank stares, and some are oblivious to the fact that half the class doesn't want to hear what they are about to say and the other half probably already knows exactly what they are going to say.

Anyway, as soon as they turn to face the class, they see me and make some sort of effort to introduce me to the class. I'm guessing a good quarter of the kids in each class have already endured this in another period and are probably as tired of it as I am, but the show must go on.

Each teacher says, "Mr. Locke?" Then I answer, "Yes," and then they say something like, "We are so happy to have you and your father join our school. I hear you are quite the wrestler." By the time I have done this three or four times, I am no longer even remotely entertained by it and barely acknowledge what they say. I don't want to be rude exactly; I'm just getting numb to it all.

When the bell rings, I glance at my schedule to see that next up is lunch. Well, that's a refreshing break from this meet and greet parade. I'll take it.

Of course, being a teacher's kid, I pretty much get whatever hot lunch they are serving for free, so whatever that happens to be today will have to work.

This time, Captain America and Jess are nowhere to be found, so I guess they either don't have lunch now or are already in the cafeteria. That's fine by me. I could use a little bit of alone time.

As I have been all day, I follow the crowd to lunch, and as I see the line stretching outside the doors to the cafeteria, I can also smell something pretty pungent coming from inside. I take a quick look at the menu posted outside. *Goulash.* Yep, that's exactly the smell I am picking up, so that mystery is solved. My stomach turns a little knowing that this is going to be a challenge—choking down some slop.

There are a few people pushing and joking around in line, and several are pointing in my direction and either laughing or quickly looking the other way when they see me looking back at them. It's a slow line, but I don't know whether that's because the kids are being stupid or they are all just taking their sweet time, dreading the upcoming culinary delight. It's becoming clear that whenever I do get my food, I'm going to have to choke it down pretty quickly. It won't have much time to settle either, because I have PE right after this with Coach, and there is no chance he is going to go easy on me. That's one thing I can always count on.

I finally get my lunch then scan the room, looking for what I hope is a quiet spot where I can eat this stuff as fast as possible without tasting any of it, if I can. I start to my left then turn back abruptly in the direction I came from when that book nerd bumps into me *again*. This time, he sends my tray smashing into my shirt with slop sliding down the front of me.

I immediately react, popping back my hips as quickly as possible, but the damage is done. I feel the blood rushing to my head and my heart pumping a little faster. I am going to go off on this turd immediately.

39

"Watch it, nerd!" I shout, staring straight into his eyes and letting him know that I can reach in and pull his soul right out of his body if I need to. I am standing there with crap on my shirt, everyone staring, and I am pissed.

Without thinking, I reach out and give him a shove that sends him spiraling backward until he lands on the table behind him, sitting on a fresh tray of goulash. This seems like justice being served, really, but I can't stop there, not with everyone looking.

"You better stay out of my way, nerd, or you're gonna seriously regret it. That is the second time today you bumped into me, and there won't be a third, got it?" I warn, my finger in his face.

By this point, the kid is practically shaking and can't get his hands up fast enough to ask for mercy that he is simply not going to get from me.

I see a banana on the table and, not caring at all who it belongs to, I grab it and start peeling as I storm off. I cannot wait to get to gym class to let off some steam. I don't even care what we're doing. Whatever it is, I'm going to give it one hundred percent and try to calm down as much as possible so I can have half a chance of getting through this day without going completely ballistic on some unsuspecting dude then have to deal with the wrath of Coach for the rest of the evening and throughout the night. I'm pretty sure he doesn't want me drawing that kind of attention to him or our "family" on the first day.

Wrestling a Demon

Jon

AFTER CAUSING DUSTIN to dump his goulash all over himself, I am now somehow sitting directly on top of a lunch tray, and there is no way that standing up isn't going to be a massive embarrassment. I can feel the warmth through my jeans, which is more than enough to cause me to lose my appetite. Thankfully, I have PE right after lunch—a vomiting accident waiting to happen, normally. This time, it is good since I can get out of the hot lunch pants that I am wearing.

Marc does his best to help me up and conceal as much of the mess on my pants as possible. Of course, as I hurry out of the lunch room, it literally erupts with laughter. It's the kind of laughter that makes you want to shrink down to the size of an ant and scurry away as fast as possible. Yeah, this day keeps getting better and better by the minute. More like more and more awful!

As soon as I get to the locker room, there is a note up that says all PE classes will be held in the wrestling room, so we have to get changed and report there for class. Of course. Now I'm going to get the pleasure of getting my butt kicked by literally any boy or girl in the class who is fortunate enough to be paired with me for whatever barbaric drills we are going to have to endure for an hour. I cannot wait.

When Marc and I get to the wrestling room, as I feared, it is partner drills. However, I am possibly in luck because, as expected, Coach Locke is pairing us up by weight. Marc and I are pretty much the same weight, so the best-case scenario is that the two of us will do the drills together.

Both of us are feeling good about this strategy as we try to stay together and hope that Coach Locke makes us an easy matchup.

As this is happening, Coach Locke looks over at the door and says, "You're late!"

The reply comes as Dustin walks into the room. "Yeah, I had a bit of an accident in the lunch room."

Oh no, this cannot be happening!

Coach Locke tells him, "Go partner up with one of the guys near your weight."

Dustin looks over and sees me. "I think he looks like exactly my weight."

I look left then right, and then down. All hope that he was pointing at someone else is lost. Great, I am going to get the pleasure of becoming a pretzel for the great state champion wrestler for the next hour.

Of course every drill that Coach Locke wants us to execute requires a demonstration and, since Dustin knows all the drills, the two of us get to be the guinea pigs. I should say that Dustin is demonstrating the moves and I am flopping around like a cheap store mannequin that is barely able to keep all their limbs attached. I lose a shoe here and the other there, and barely avoid having my shorts pulled down to my knees as Dustin repeatedly throws me and pins me to the ground.

After forty-five minutes of playing rag doll with me, I can see he is starting to smile and feel a little better. How nice for him! I am proportionally feeling worse and worse and quickly realizing that tomorrow is going to be fundamentally full of aches and pains in places that I never even knew existed.

Then I have a bright idea. I raise my hand and ask, "Coach Locke, could I please use the restroom?"

"Just this one time, Bragg. Next time, make sure you go potty before coming to my class. That goes for all of you, got it?"

Everyone nods. Nobody wants to become the wrestling dummy for an Olympic champion.

I have literally no idea why it took me so long to come up with the obvious solution, but I nod violently in agreement and head for the locker room as fast as possible to try to sell the fact that I cannot hold it in a second longer. I mean, the relief I feel is almost instantaneous as I narrowly escape that class with all my limbs intact.

As I am making my way out of the wrestling room, I hear several other people latch onto my little scheme and also ask to go to the bathroom. Since Coach Locke already established the precedent by allowing me to go, he pretty much has to let the other kids go until he is basically left with members of the wrestling team.

I mean, unlike the rest of us, it makes sense for them to go through the drills. I cannot think of one time when I intend to use anything that he is teaching us about wrestling. I most certainly am not going to ever try out for the wrestling team, and I don't plan on getting into a scuffle of any kind with anyone ever. I am simply not a fighter. I know a lot of people say they are a lover, not a fighter, but I'm actually neither. I am simply a person who prefers to avoid pain and to keep my body in as good of a functioning state as possible, given my obvious lack of physical fitness. I don't see any reason why I should waste any of my time focusing on how to escape a particular wrestling move that puts me into a position that I never plan on getting into.

Unlike most of the classes at school, I don't see how gym is going to be helpful in my future life or professional career.

I am going to make this trip to the bathroom take as long as possible, even if I have to wash my hands ten times and wait for the obnoxiously loud and forceful hand dryer to finish its job over and over again. After all, your hands can never really be too dry, can they?

Nothing Special

Dustin

WHEN I STORMED INTO the locker room with goulash all over my shirt, I saw the note that all gym classes would be held in the wrestling room. That was finally some good news. I would be able to take out my frustrations on some poor sucker who would have to deal with the fact that I am in a dangerous, violent mood right now.

First, I had to spend a few minutes trying to scrape the crap off my shirt and pants and into the nearest trash can. Of course I got the chunks off, but there is no way that stain is going to come clean without a washing machine. This means I am going to have to hear it from Coach when I get home about taking better care of my clothes.

Coach is one of those guys who you would expect to be ex-military, but maybe it's years and years of wrestling coaches yelling at him, or his mashed-up cauliflower ears. Either way, he likes things kept a certain way.

All the dishes are stacked perfectly in our cupboards, all the cans are neatly placed in the pantry with all the labels facing outward and spaced evenly apart. Even the refrigerator is organized into compartments to keep things nice and tidy so he knows where to find everything. I don't exactly know what my punishment is going to be for staining these clothes, but there will undoubtedly be negative consequences and a life lesson to learn.

On top of this looming over my head, I ended up running late for PE class. Coach would definitely have a problem with that, too. At this point, I' wasn't sure it mattered that much. How much worse could it be?

When I attempted to sneak into the wrestling room, Coach met me at the door to inform me that I was late and that I needed to partner up with someone my weight.

I looked around the room and, to my great surprise and satisfaction, Bragg was in this class. Without blinking an eye, I quickly pointed him out, making sure he knew he was going to be my victim—I mean, partner—for whatever drills Coach had in mind. I certainly hoped they were reasonably violent. Even if they were not, they would be today.

Bragg and his buddy, Thor, did try their best to avoid me picking them, but I could see Bragg's eyes drop when he came to the realization that any discussion was pointless because Coach was going to let me do what I wanted.

Since Coach is looking for me to test the students, I can definitely use that as an excuse to get a little aggressive with everyone, but Bragg is the only one I really want to put through the wringer.

So, we now spend a little bit of time learning basic moves, throws, and escapes. I gladly volunteer to show everyone how to do each and every move as slowly and painfully as possible for my partner. It's just so perfect and poetic justice that this worked out so well for me.

After about fifteen minutes of drilling, Coach decides to let us free roll, which means we are able to wrestle one-on-one with timed rounds. I think I must have pinned Bragg in under thirty seconds every single round, and then we reset over and over again for me to pin him yet again.

By the time we are halfway through the class, I am so enjoying this period. I can tell it's taking a toll on Bragg—he's going slower and slower and making less and less effort to avoid his next loss. That doesn't matter to me at all. I keep going faster and faster and harder and harder. It feels great!

Then, when class is nearing an end, as if a light bulb goes off in that nerdy little head of his, Bragg asks Coach if he can go to the bathroom. I'm sure he doesn't really need to go to the bathroom but, at this point, I'm almost tired of kicking his butt and am ready to actually wrestle with someone.

After the rest of the people, who have no business being in the wrestling room, all go to the bathroom, we are down to those who are either on the wrestling team or want to be. Everything gets a bit more boring at this point, because beating them up isn't as much fun as getting revenge on Bragg.

When the period ends, Coach calls me over and asks, "What did you think of the Bragg kid?"

My response is simple. "Well, he doesn't have anything to brag about, that's for sure. There is nothing special about him." I mean that, too. Bragg not only repeatedly got pinned, he was significantly out of breath and virtually unable to pick himself up off the mat, let alone represent any sort of challenge to me. He definitely is not what Coach is looking for, which is someone with a natural ability above and beyond normal. Unless it's the ability to repeatedly get your lunch handed to you. In that case, then and only then is Bragg special.

With that, Coach dismisses me. "Okay, just keep an eye out like we talked about. Someone really smart or someone who is even naturally musical could be of interest."

I nod my head, confirming that I will do my best to keep my eyes open. It's unlikely, though, that I am going to see too much for the rest of the day, stuck in a classroom with a bunch of sophomores who pretty much only want to send each other text messages all throughout class and/or sleep for hours and hours on end. I don't really blame them. This is the sleepy part of the day, after eating lunch, not wearing a lunch, and getting a solid workout in. A little shut-eye can be nice. Too bad I don't have any study halls lined up.

Instead, I head to one of my least favorite classes—Algebra. Hating it is largely due to the fact that I don't get the practicality of the Pythagorean Theorem and logarithmic functions, or whatever they are called.

As I settle in for a nice little snooze after the latest redundant introduction of my presence to the class, my attention turns to Mrs. Greene, our Algebra teacher. She has gray hair pulled up into a bun, an unusually long, tan wool dress, sensible tan working shoes, and the kind of voice that makes you think she smoked three packs of cigarettes a day at some point in her long, sorted life. She is going on and on saying, "My mother's age, divided by five, is equal to my sister's age, divided by three. My sister is three years older than me. My mother's age is three less than two times my age. How old is my mother?"

Um, the answer is: who cares? Yeah, this is going to be a riveting class in the lazy part of the afternoon, for sure.

As I get ready to drift off, I notice I am not the only person who is not paying attention. I see a relatively normal-looking guy sitting a couple of rows over, clearly watching a movie on his phone. Ha, yeah, that is a pretty good idea, if I don't say so myself. I am quite impressed by the audacity of this dude, so that gets my attention as I stare for an uneasy amount of time, trying to figure out what movie he is streaming. In fact, I am so engrossed in this that I jump half out of my seat when Mrs. Greene slaps a pop quiz on my desk.

"Let's see how much you learned from the example that I just went over, Mr. Locke."

There's a shock. Not paying attention has bit me in the butt again.

I stare at the page for a good five minutes when I notice movement from the movie guy. He gets up, takes his paper to the front, and drops it off on Mrs. Greene's desk before he walks out the door. How is he able to just leave class like that?

"Excellent work yet again, Mr. Ryan," Mrs. Greene tells him, but he is already gone.

That was ... unexpected. He must be some sort of a math whiz or something. I am definitely going to start sitting next to him in this class, that's for sure.

Saved by the Bell

Jon

THANKFULLY, THE REST of the school day is relatively easily, split between Study Hall, Spanish, and Home Economics. I'm ready for a nice break from what has been one hot mess of a birthday, though I was able to read several chapters of *Romeo and Juliet* in Study Hall and managed to make it through Spanish, Home Economics, and several hallway shuffles without running into Dustin again, literally. That is certainly a good thing. I clearly have already used up all my allowed accidental encounters with that guy.

It usually takes me a lot longer to annoy people than one day, but I guess Dustin just got lucky. I definitely earned my reputation for being a clumsy book nerd who is afraid of his own shadow.

I finally stop holding my breath at the end of the day and truly feel saved by the bell. I am even super happy to see Mom wildly waving at us in the pickup line. At least someone is glad to see us today.

I didn't have my final period with Marc, so we have to wait a bit for him to arrive before we can head out. Since it's my birthday, Marc is going to come over for dinner and some semblance of a birthday celebration with my family then a sleepover. I don't really do big parties and never have. My parents started early on with that, saying we could invite one friend over. Otherwise, birthday celebrations are kept to the family. That's fine by me. I really didn't want to have to decide who should get an invite or not from my classes in school while growing up.

As far as I can tell, in high school, there are two kinds of birthday parties. The ones that include just your family, and then there are the raging parties with alcohol, music, and things I will never know about since I don't get invited. That is generally reserved for the jocks and popular kids. Once again, that is all fine with me. I have no desire to lose control over my body or my ability to think clearly. I don't see the point, to be honest, and I feel like it is nothing but a disadvantage. In fact, since my mind is likely my only real advantage, if anything, I would like to boost that versus putting a damper on it by drinking.

So, anyway, Marc is coming home with us, and it doesn't take long before I spot his curly hair and blue backpack making its way over to our van. He seems to be in a pretty good mood. I'm almost certain it's because he enjoys a good birthday party and sleepover.

Okay, I know I'm sixteen, but every once in a while, Marc and I crash at each other's houses and either play video games or talk about what we are going to do when we grow up. We have also been known to binge-watch some of our favorite shows and pull an all-nighter, lost in some television world. That is unlikely to happen tonight, since we have school tomorrow, but I know it's going to be fun anyway.

Marc gets to the van and says, "Hey, it's the birthday boy! Are you ready to party?"

This gives all of us a good laugh, knowing that is not going to happen.

Still, I confirm by saying, "You know it!"

We laugh a bit more as we head out of the parking lot and on to the next adventure of the day—heading over to the middle school to pick up Jill. As usual, she is simply standing there, waiting for us as if she has been waiting for a million years. It's not really her fault. I do the same thing when I'm waiting to get picked up. It goes on like this until you relinquish control over it and find more useful things to do with the extra time. For me, it's reading my latest book, but Jill hasn't quite found her distraction yet. So, she waits impatiently every day.

After we pick Jill up and before we get too far, I notice we aren't going in the direction of our house.

"Where are we going?" I ask Mom.

"I ordered you a birthday cake this year, since I didn't have time to make one with all the activity today, so we're going to run by the store to pick it up."

Interesting. With everything going on at our house—whatever that might be—Mom is willing to give up on some of our traditions. I have to admit I am going to miss her homemade angel food cake this year, but I'm sure whatever we get at the store will be fine.

We pull into the parking lot of the grocery store, and Mom and Jill head in while Marc and I continue discussing the crazy events of the day.

"How about Dustin?" Marc asks. "I'm pretty sure he already hates both of us for some reason."

"Oh, I think he has a pretty good reason to not like me after bumping into him multiple times today. I do think he is a little overzealous, though. Did you see him rag doll me in gym class?" I exclaim, rubbing my already sore back.

"Sorry about that, but I sure did. All I kept thinking was how glad I was it wasn't me."

I have to laugh at that. You see, Marc and I are always honest with each other, and so I have to agree that, if it was him partnering up with Dustin, I would have felt the same relief.

It takes a little while at the store, so while we wait, we end up listening to the radio. The news is on the investigation into what happened to Coach Keith. They are still trying to figure out exactly what type of animal killed him and are not having any luck tracking anything down. Nobody has seen any bears roaming around and, other than several deer, which definitely could not have done this, most of the animals are way too small to have carried out this gruesome of an attack on a grown man like Mr. Keith. They say the investigation is ongoing, and if anyone knows anything about what happened, they are urged to contact the Grinwell Police Department.

Finally, Mom and Jill exit the store. Jill seems fine, but Mom does not look happy at all, which tells me something else didn't go as planned today. They get in the car, and Mom starts with, "Perfect, just perfect. They somehow confirmed my order yet never actually made the cake. I tried to get any type of cake they might have available to see if they could make something work, but the best they could do is cupcakes. I'm so sorry, Jon-boy."

Poor Mom looks close to tears, so I assure her. "It's fine, Mom. Don't worry about it. Cupcakes are just as good as cake. I'm sure it will be fine."

"Thank you. I just wanted your sixteenth birthday to be special, I'm so disappointed the cake I ordered didn't get done."

I reach around the driver's seat to give her a seat hug and thank her for the effort. It's not her fault that the bakery messed up the order. She's a pretty great mom. I have to admit that I got really lucky in the parent lottery, that's for sure. Both Mom and Dad are fantastic parents.

The Bleachers

Dustin

THE AFTERNOON HAS BEEN crawling by as I sit through the rest of the classes, staring at the clock and waiting for the bell. So, before the last bell of the day even rings, I am already standing up and on my way out the door. I know exactly where I need to go next—wrestling practice.

I head to the coaches' area and try to find the office that has been assigned to Coach. It's pretty easy to spot, as it has some streamers and a big welcome sign on the front of the door.

I step inside the office and see that it barely qualifies as an office, despite the fact that there are four walls behind the one door. The back wall is painted in the school's bright orange color and made of concrete blocks, like I imagine you would find in a prison or old hospital, at best, and they are cold because it is winter and, well, it's Iowa.

For whatever reason, Coach is not there, so I decide to cop a squat in his chair to see what the old man has been up to.

I sit there for a few minutes before I decide to check in the drawers to see if he has any snacks squirreled away yet. Of course not. Then I open the bottom drawer and see a row of files with student names on them. It's parted near the front, and I see the name *Jon Bragg*. *Ha*, this should be entertaining.

I pull out the folder, expecting to see perfect grades and other school-type papers. Instead, a few photos fall out and hit the floor. I reach down to scoop them up.

They are old pictures of Bragg and what looks like his family. Whatever. I don't really care.

Just as I am sliding those back into the folder, I hear Coach clear his throat and say, "Can I help you?"

I look up and tell him, "I stopped by to see what drills you wanted to start practice with today, Coach."

He looks me in the eye. "For you, Locke, you can run the bleachers one hundred times in the gym. I'll run the team through the drills today."

"Why? That's not fair!" I complain.

He looks me straight in the eyes like he is staring into the back of my head. "Stay. Out. Of. My. Stuff." He stresses every single word. Then, to emphasize it, he forcefully raises his hand and points in the direction of the gym.

Perfect.

I head to the locker room to get my workout clothes back on, grumbling all the way. What is his problem? I wish Coach could just lighten up for a minute. Then I head to the gym and begin the punishment—I mean, my workout.

As I run up the bleachers, I am immediately annoyed, especially because these are old wooden bleachers, the kind that slide out from the wall. In case you have never had to run bleachers before, it means you go up the bleachers on the far left, run across the top all the way to the right, and then run down, just to start the process all over again, running a giant circle. He says to do it one hundred times, but I know that means I am to keep running until he comes get me. There is no way I am going to finish running these before wrestling practice is over. He only uses this particular punishment to drive a point home.

The most annoying part of this is every step you take sounds like a bass drum being struck as hard as possible, and then it rattles like a thousand cymbals—incredibly loud with no way to avoid that so it is painfully clear to anyone near the gym that someone is being taught a lesson.

As I run, I don't get tired at all. Instead, I get angry. Why did he have to move us from my old school where I had a ton of friends and had already established myself as the big man on campus? Now I have to start all over again in this stupid small town with a bunch of ridiculous kids who are really starting to get on my nerves. Coach gets all the accolades and kind words, and everyone is so excited to have "Mr. Olympian" swooping in to save the wrestling team. Yet I am the one who is going to have to do all of the work.

Somehow, I am going to have to take this bunch of losers on the team and turn them into winners, because we all know that all Coach is going to do is repeatedly yell at them. I'm the one who is going to have to throw them on my back and lead this group of Tigers to victory. We all know that I am the only high caliber wrestler on the team and that everyone else is average at best. It's so annoying.

I push harder and harder, and the racket gets louder and louder as I pick up the pace.

Before I know it, Coach comes running in and is yelling at me, "What are you doing? You need to slow down. You are drawing too much attention and are going to burn off all that energy that I pumped into you this morning."

I think to myself, *Whatever*. However, I reply, "I am barely breaking a sweat, Coach."

"I know, and that's the problem." He glares at me. "Since you have so much energy, you can run yourself home. We will see how you feel after that."

"Fine!" I yell at him. "You are such an overreacting jackass!"

"We will talk about this when you get home. Don't be late for dinner!"

Now I get to throw my clothes into my backpack, throw my backpack on my back, and run all the way home in the middle of winter. Yep, this is just the perfect first day at a new school. Welcome to my new life in this frozen little town with this impossible to please tyrant ruining my life.

You know what? I don't even care. Not even a little bit. I'm certainly not going to give him the satisfaction of knowing he caused me to break. Nope. I am just going to suck it up and see him back at that crap hole of a house we live in now.

Surprise

Jon

WHEN WE PULL INTO OUR driveway, Mom reaches up to press the button to open the garage door. That's when I see something is definitely off.

"Oh yeah, I forgot to tell you," Mom says. "All of Grandpa and Grandma's stuff is in the garage."

The garage is bursting with boxes, and there is no place for either my mom or dad to park their cars. That is unexpected, but it does explain Mom and Dad's choice of clothing this morning and the work they were planning for today.

I still can't stop wondering how all this happened without me being involved in helping them move. Actually, I'm okay with that. I got lucky there, not having to carry box after box out of Grandma and Grandpa's house, into a truck, and then back out of the truck and into our garage. That's not my idea of a good time. Although, I am a bit intrigued by what might be in those boxes.

Grandpa and Grandma have some pretty cool antiques and some really interesting books in their library. I sure hope they brought those. I would love to read them.

I snap out of that train of thought and collect my school stuff and the handful of groceries that Mom did get while she was at the store. Then Mom, Marc, Jill, and I walk through the back door, which leads straight into the kitchen.

I love this kitchen, even though it may be a little dated. It has orange countertops and avocado appliances, all of which are originals from when the house was built in the 1970s. In fact, they are so old that now they are classics, I think, and back in style.

I see Mom has indeed brought Marc's balloons and planted them around the dinner table. That is always fun because, as you eat, your head gets bopped repeatedly by the balloons when the furnace kicks on and off. It doesn't matter to me either way. I am glad to be home and looking forward to kicking back, playing some video games, and then relaxing in my room.

I turn the corner and head up the stairs toward my room, motioning for Marc to follow. First, I am going to change. I still have a bit of lunch stains going on, and I want to be more comfortable.

As I open the door to my room, I immediately notice something is different. My room has been a bit rearranged, and half the room now has another bed and an old dresser and nightstand that are familiar-looking. The realization hits me like a ton of bricks. Grandpa is here already and not just all his and Grandma's stuff.

I turn around to yell downstairs, but Mom is already hot on my heels.

"Jon, I was going to tell you in the car, but I got caught up in the cake fiasco. Grandpa is also here and down in the living room."

"Okay, I should probably go down and talk to him."

She shrugs. "You can try, but he isn't really talking right now."

After changing really quick, I head downstairs again to see Grandpa, also known as my new roommate.

As soon as I get to the living room, I see him. He is sitting in a wheelchair, which I have never seen him do before, staring blankly out the window and mumbling something. It's hard to watch.

"Grandpa?" I say quietly.

He turns and looks at me, and then his eyes light up as if he is happy to see me and he says, "I once heard some words that unlocked my brain. It cleared up the fog so I could think again."

I turn to Mom and Marc and shrug. Then I turn back to Grandpa and tell him, "Okay, Grandpa, sounds good." For some reason, I then talk louder and state, "It looks like you and me are going to be roommates. Welcome to our home, Grandpa!"

He keeps mumbling the same thing over and over again, but he gets quieter and quieter each time until he turns back toward the window and falls back into staring at whatever he is looking at outside.

I can't help but immediately feel a sense of loss. I have never seen anyone like this, let alone my grandpa. He is unquestionably not all there. It's a bit overwhelming.

The only thing I can think to do is head over to my mom and fall into her open arms. She pats me on the back of the head a bit and then, after a minute, pulls back a little to tell me, "I know it's difficult, Jon-boy, but we are doing everything we can to help Grandpa. The doctors say he should be okay, but he isn't responding to any treatments or medicine."

"I feel so bad for him," I tell her. "I'm glad he's here so we can take care of him. I promise I'll do whatever I can."

"We know, Jon-boy. Thank you for being so understanding. Love you, son."

"Love you, too," I tell her then look over at Marc and realize he is trying to take all this in. Then he nods back. He understands.

Without saying a word, we both head over to where the game console is so we can spend some time mindlessly playing video games and trying to shake what we just witnessed, as well as the effects of a pretty rough school day.

We have been playing for a few minutes when Marc says, "What did your grandpa say to you?"

"Honestly, I'm not sure, but it sounded like some sort of a poem, I think. It must be from one of his old books. I didn't recognize it."

"Yeah, I have never heard anyone talk like that."

I agree. "Neither have I."

We decide then to focus on our favorite battle royale and see if we can manage to last longer than the other random people who have joined our game lobby. That's the awesome thing about video games. You can play with completely random strangers and still have a ton of fun just trying to outlast them, running around and hiding, or going on the offensive in whatever world the game developer has constructed for you. It's a mostly equal playing field where size doesn't matter, but strategic thinking and experience pays off, allowing you to last longer and ultimately to be the last man standing at the end of the game. Marc and I are good at these games and are getting well-known in our gaming circle for being a duo you want to break up early. They can try.

Extra Homework

Dustin

AFTER A GOOD SEVEN mile run, I finally make it home to our little house in the country, which sits in a field well back from the road to give us a bit of privacy. The air outside has the constant smell of manure from a pig farm about a mile south of us that has a surprisingly potent range for the fumes. The only thing worse than stepping outside in the morning to smell this is breathing it in as you run the last couple of miles. It literally smells exactly like most of this day has been and actually sums the whole thing up quite well.

As I step inside the house, the smell shifts from pig crap to the liver and onions that Coach has prepared for dinner. He knows how much I detest liver, so I'm sure he chose this meal just to get further under my skin. However, I am not going to give him the pleasure of knowing he accomplished that, even if I have to choke down a whole pound of liver. I am going to sit there and eat it like it is the best cut of steak cooked to perfection by a famous chef. I will force back the gagging sensation that springs up from my stomach, through my throat, and literally smile as I look him straight in the eye.

He hears me step into the house and says, "Locke, I made liver and onions, your personal favorite." He laughs.

"Sounds great. I could eat a horse."

I can tell he is a little disappointed by my response but not totally sold on my statement.

I don't even bother showering or changing; I step right up to the table and have a seat.

61

Coach comes in and joins me, still wearing a cocky grin on his face, expecting me to break at any second.

I look at the pile of charred meat and grilled onions in front of me and cut a big old bite, chew it slowly, and swallow like I am savoring every second of this not-so-fine meal.

I repeat this for several bites before he finally gives in and says, "Impressive. You are learning how to use psychology to conquer your own emotions and to strategically defeat your opponent. Nice job."

I choke a little, not because of the meat but because that sounded like a sincere compliment and was truly unexpected.

At this point, he straightens up and is all business again. "Okay, so, today we at least learned that Jon Bragg is not interesting to us. You wrestled him and felt nothing at all, so we can go ahead and ignore him for now."

"Fine by me. The less I see of him, the better. Otherwise, I might have to punch him in the face."

Coach Locke chuckles. "So, that leaves us with about half a dozen other students who might be of interest. I have their files right here."

"I actually think that Brad Dillon and Jess Friggens might have something special about them, especially Brad. I mean, he was a true freshman last year when he earned the varsity starting quarterback job; that's pretty special."

"And why Jess?" he asks.

"I have a feeling about her, like I am drawn to her like every other guy in the school, but maybe even a little more."

"Interesting," Coach says. "Okay, spend some time researching Dillon and Friggens. I also want you to study all the student records for the guys on the wrestling team."

Oh boy, that is going to ruin what was left of a perfectly disappointing day.

I think about it for a minute, but I really don't have anything to lose, and I'm tired of doing this type of thing. "Why don't you just tell me why we are doing this and exactly what we are looking for in these prospects?"

"I have been waiting for you to finally get the guts to ask me, Locke. Maybe you aren't a lost cause after all. Follow me downstairs."

We go into the basement where there are a bunch of really old containers. There is also an old freezer, which he opens. That's when I see a few rows of frozen blue liquid in glass vials. This is where the blue serum he gives me every week is coming from.

He points. "You see that?"

I nod.

"I know you love the way it makes you feel, but, well, we are almost completely out of it."

I immediately start thinking to myself, *Well, that's a cool story, but who cares?*

"You are probably wondering why this is relevant. Well, it comes from extracting the blood from special people like us, and then filtering their blue essence out of the blood through a special process that has been handed down through our family for generations. There are only a handful of people in the world, at any point in time, who have blood with the properties we need to produce our blue essence."

Okay, now I am completely grossed out.

"What? That stuff is some sort of blood juice?"

"No," he calmly says. "I said it is a *filtered* solution that purifies the blood and turns it into this blue liquid, which has to stay extremely cold to keep its vitality."

I feel a bit like I have been punched in the gut and lost all my wind.

"So, what you're saying is that I have been cheating? How is that possible? I have been tested for performance enhancing drugs several times, and everything was okay. Was everything I accomplished last year a complete scam?"

He shakes his head. "No, that is not how it works. Just like only a few people have the properties in their blood, only a few people can react to the purified solution. It cannot be detected, because it is natural. And to be completely clear, it is not man-made."

I throw my hands up, struggling a bit to catch my breath and calm my heart rate down. I'm still not following what is going on here.

"Dustin, we are far removed descendants of a people from Asgard."

"Stop messing around," I scoff. "Are you talking about Thor and Loki fantasies? Get real with me."

"In fact," he continues, "you and I do come from Loki's line. You see, the way this works is pretty simple. An heir to the bloodline of anyone from Asgard can inherit some, or all, of the abilities of the Asgardian that he or she comes from."

I look at him like he is crazy. "You have got to be kidding me!"

"I'm afraid not, Locke. And, in our case, due to an unjust punishment handed down by a group of rogue, do-gooder Asgardians ages ago that drained our line, we can only keep some semblance of our power through drinking this blue serum. Otherwise, we will lose our abilities and return to being fully human. "

I shake my head.

"How do you think you suddenly flipped a switch when you turned sixteen and went from being the worst wrestler in your weight class to winning state in the same year?"

Well, that's a solid argument. I was indeed one of the lucky ones who unexpectedly seemed to outperform beyond anyone's wildest expectations, but I wouldn't say I was the *worst*.

"Without this blue liquid, all of that will go away," Coach says slowly and clearly to emphasize his point.

I have a sudden feeling of desperation because, at this point, I cannot be exposed as a fraud or a cheater. I am in this thing too deep. Plus, I don't want to become a loser, a weakling, and I … I'm just not going to let that happen, period.

I look at him with resolve in my eyes. "Well, we have no choice then. We have to find someone so we can continue what we have started, because I am *not* going back to normal." I hesitate, but I think it is important to ask, "So, your win at the Olympics was because of this?"

He nods. "I'm afraid so, Locke. At least now you know why you have to work with me to find someone fast. I know there is at least one person from Asgard in this town. I have traced all the families, and there is definitely a descendant here."

I back out of the basement and head upstairs to get some air and to think. I mean, it's completely crazy to consider this story could actually be true, but I have to admit that Coach hasn't ever lied to me.

It certainly is strange that I made so much progress in a year, and it is also true that it coincided with when I turned sixteen and started drinking the blue stuff. Whatever it is and wherever it comes from, I really don't want to run out of it all of a sudden.

I have a new mission in life—find someone special. And, apparently, someone with an Asgardian ancestor here at this school. It just has to be Captain America. I need to find out tomorrow. Nothing is more important to me from this point going forward. My whole world has changed.

I guess I am like some sort of Asgardian junkie or something. This is unreal but also kind of cool. I mean, Loki is cool, right?

Candles

Jon

AS IT USUALLY HAPPENS, Marc and I get lost in the game and, before we know it, Mom calls, "Dinner! Wash up and come to the table, boys."

I hear Jill moving around upstairs and look up at the clock, realizing I am pretty hungry.

Marc and I announce to our allies that we are leaving the game and bow out as gracefully as we can. Then I shut off the game console and stand up, suddenly remembering my little wrestling encounter with Dustin as my body screams with aches and pains that were long forgotten in the virtual world.

I grimace and say, "Man, I am really sore from gym class today. I sure hope we don't do wrestling for too long, or if we do, you and I have to figure out a way to partner up. No more Dustin for me."

"Yeah, I don't want any part of that. It looked like it sucked, for sure. Sorry about that, Jon."

I shrug. It's water under the bridge at this point. "It's okay. It is what it is. Let's eat."

I smell something amazing coming from the kitchen and, after a second of processing, I figure out it is spaghetti and meatballs, my favorite meal. Now, that is what I am talking about!

To me, that dinner is what my birthday is all about. I cannot wash up and get to the dining room fast enough.

When we get there, I see that Mom or Dad have wheeled Grandpa in and decide to try again.

"Grandpa, you're going to love Mom's spaghetti. It's the best!"

He doesn't look up but mumbles again, "I once heard some words that ..."

I can't make the rest out, but I nod at him then look at Mom. "Thank you for making this, Mom!"

"You're welcome, Jon-boy. I know it's your favorite. Happy birthday!"

I smile like I have never smiled before, so happy and feeling so fortunate in the moment. Then, for the next fifteen or twenty minutes, there isn't much talking going on as we all focus on devouring two giant bowls of spaghetti. It's so good. Gradually, each person taps out until we all are sitting there with our forks down and a content look on our faces. That. Was. Amazing.

"Son," Dad says, "we know things are different this year, but we want to keep our family traditions, so it's your birthday and it's time for each of us to say something we love about the birthday boy. I'll start."

I have to admit that I do like this part of my birthday.

He looks around the table then continues, "I really appreciate your kindness and how much you care about this family. With things like sharing your room with Grandpa and just being there for him, that's truly a gift, son."

I swell up a little bit with pride. After a rough day, it feels good to get some praise and positive feedback.

Mom decides to go next. "I love how interested you are in books and poetry. I also love to read your poetry. It really is beautiful. I know you are going to do something amazing with it in your future."

I blush a little. I have always been shy about my writing and, well, I don't know about all that future talk. I'm not sure how special it is either compared to all the classic books I have read and the talented authors that I love. It's hard to imagine ever getting close to that level of writing perfection. I'm also sure that this means Mom has been poking around in my bedroom and most likely read through my poetry journal. I guess that's okay. I mean, I don't have anything to hide from her.

It's Jill's turn, and I know that this pains her quite a bit—having to try to come up with something nice. I feel the same way on her birthday, so it is completely understood. It's not that we don't love or appreciate each other, but we naturally bounce back and forth between love and hate on a daily basis, being siblings and all.

She sees everyone staring at her, and the silence grows more awkward by the second. She finally caves and says, "Okay, okay. I appreciate it when you put the toilet seat down after going to the bathroom, and that you don't leave the bathroom a mess."

Whoa! This is high praise coming from Jill. I mean, I mostly do it because I don't like it messy, and I don't want to accidentally sit on a wet seat in the middle of the night. So, keeping the bathroom, and especially the toilet, clean is kind of self-serving, but I will take the compliment.

Even though he doesn't have to partake in this, Marc is all too eager to offer a compliment tonight, as well. "I appreciate how good of a friend you are, and how you took on the state wrestling champ today so I didn't have to. Now that's a great friend!"

Mom, Dad, and Jill exchange blank expressions, which Marc and I get a kick out of.

I have to laugh at that, even though not everyone around the table fully appreciates it. "You owe me for that one, for sure."

He nods in agreement and repeatedly pats me on the back, agreeing physically that he owes me one.

We skip Grandpa, since he doesn't seem too interested in what we are doing. So, now it's my turn to talk as the birthday boy. I thank everyone, saying, "I feel so blessed to be a part of our family. Thank you all for the kind words, especially Jill. I know that had to hurt a little."

Everyone laughs, except Jill. She nods, but then gives in and smiles.

I continue, "This has been the best part of the day by far. So, how about dessert?"

Mom and Dad get up to head to the kitchen to get the cupcakes. When they come out, I see they have put all of them on a cookie sheet and arranged them into the number sixteen with as many candles on them. They sing "Happy Birthday" again, but this time with a lot more pep than they did this morning.

When Mom sets the cupcakes down in front of me, I pause and make a wish. Then I proceed to blow out all the candles to a round of applause.

I don't really know if wishes come true or why that ever became a thing, but it's a nice thought. Plus, I might as well give it a go.

I look over at Grandpa, and I think everyone knows what I wished for instantly. I miss him being fully present so much.

Student Records

Dustin

I GO BACK UPSTAIRS after Coach's revelation and grab the files that he brought home with him, taking them to my room. I need some time and some space from Coach to take all of this in and process what I just heard. I'm a little bit numb to it right now and still trying to decide how much of it I believe. I guess, instinctively, I know it's true, that what he said lines up with exactly what has happened to me over the last year. I still have a bunch of questions but, at this point, I'm not ready to talk to Coach, and I'm not sure how helpful he will be, anyway. I mean, he has basically been lying to the world for the entire time that I have known him, and to me for the entire time that I have been living with him again. He actually is playing with my life, really. I didn't ask for this problem, but now I am in too deep to do anything other than help him find someone special.

I wonder how all this exactly works. Do we have to kill the person once we find them? If that's the case, does Coach expect me to be okay with that? Or worse yet, do it? Also, if we kill them, wouldn't that limit the supply of blood even further? I mean, that doesn't really make sense, does it? Surely we must try to keep the person alive so they can be a continuous source of the blue essence or whatever. I guess it's also possible that there is a limited amount of the special stuff in their system, too.

You know what? I will cross those bridges when I get to them. What I know for a fact is that I need the blue stuff to continue to be a championship level wrestler, and there is no way I am going to give that up, so this search just became much more serious.

Now I also know why genealogy is so important to Coach. He has been tracking multiple family trees to try to identify people who have what both of us need to retain our added edge.

I also wonder exactly what we can do if we have enough of this blue stuff. Why do we need the blue stuff at all? Since we are descendants of people from Asgard, don't we also have this blue stuff inside of us? Maybe that is why it works on us and doesn't work on regular people who drink it. Maybe, for us, it is like topping off our tanks and giving us the extra fuel we need to be able to win. I think I might have to go down to that freezer tonight and start to experiment with this whole thing to see exactly what is possible.

One of the advantages of Coach is that he is regimented. I know for a fact that he will be lights out at ten and asleep within fifteen minutes. I need to wait for a few minutes after that, and then I can have the run of the house.

Like clockwork, Coach does his thing, and then I sneak down to the basement with a couple of small containers to grab some of the blue stuff. I am going to find out how much of this it takes for me to see noticeable changes. I think I will start tomorrow in the weight room and see how much strength I can gain if I take enough of this before heading to school in the morning. I strongly suspect Brad has something special, because he seems to have the same well above average skills and success that I have. Tomorrow morning, we will see how much above average.

I don't sleep much for the rest of the night, becoming focused on searching the web and reading up on Asgardians and the types of abilities they are supposed to have. It's hard to know what is fact versus what is purely fiction. Until a little while ago, I was pretty sure it was all fiction, so who knows?

According to most Norse mythology experts, Asgardians were supposed to have superhuman strength, speed, stamina, dense tissue, durability, healing powers, longevity, and energy manipulation powers for shapeshifting and teleportation. So, in theory, with enough of this blue stuff, I should be able to attempt all these things to see which of them are actually true and which of them are just something some writer thought of when they were creating a story.

It's a lot to process. It's essentially like having most of the good attributes of a superhero with the sad exception of the mention of flying. I guess teleportation is almost as good as flying. Maybe even better since you don't have to worry about eating any bugs or smashing into birds. That said, if we can, in fact, shapeshift, maybe we can turn into a bird or some other animal that can fly. I have no idea how I would even go about trying something like that, so I am going to put shapeshifting on hold for the more readily testable skills.

I only have a few hours before Coach expects me to head down for breakfast. I'm sure he is also going to anticipate me having a bunch of questions. Hopefully, he will add to my new supply of the blue stuff because, why not? I doubt he will, though, knowing how short we are getting on it and how we have been stretching it over the last year or so. It's going to be hard to sleep when all I really want to do is test all these ability theories out.

Tomorrow is promising to be a pretty exciting day, full of possibilities, as I explore how many powers I might have then think of the best ways to use those powers to make sure I improve the quality of my life in as many ways as possible. I know I wasn't sure at first, but now I am positive this is going to be amazing. All I really need to find out now is how amazing it will be.

Loki is such a badass, and the more I read about him, the more I like.

One Last Wish

Jon

AFTER DINNER, WE DECIDE to all watch a movie together and relax. It's not about the movie as much as it's about leaving the frustrations of the day behind us and allowing ourselves to get absorbed in something.

Ironically, this movie is about a family who goes on a vacation and, instead of flying, they decide to take a train. Everything that could go wrong does go wrong, and they end up stopping at all kinds of places along the way as the train breaks down. They experience some crazy problem or delay in each town that they stop in that requires them to work together to keep going toward their destination. In the end, they don't have time to do what they originally wanted and have to turn around and go right back. However, they don't care because they realize that spending time together was what the vacation was all about. By the end, they have so many amazing memories, having battled through things together, that the trip is a success and their family is stronger because of all they went through. Pretty cool concept.

I couldn't help but feel like what we are going through with Grandpa is a little bit like that. He is stuck in one of those small towns, taking in something amazing, and we need to find out how to get him back on track and moving in the same direction as the rest of us.

Speaking of Grandpa, we need to figure out a sleeping plan for tonight. With Grandpa in my room, that is probably going to be too tight with Marc. So, for tonight, Marc and I are going to camp out in the living room and crash on the floor in sleeping bags. We have a furnace, but since it's wintertime in Iowa, it still gets really cold at night. With the wind forcing its way through the cracks around the windows, it can get rather chilly. Fortunately, we have sleeping bags that are made for cold weather camping, so we are going to be just fine through the night. In fact, we will probably get hot in these little cocoons of ours.

Marc and I are members of the Boy Scouts, and we are both making every effort to take a run at the twenty-one merit badges needed to qualify to become Eagle Scouts. We have used these sleeping bags to earn our Backpacking, Camping, Nature, and some other badges that require us to be outdoors for an extended period of time. We have several expeditions planned for this spring and summer that should help us collect a lot more badges so we can take a run at Eagle Scout when we turn seventeen. In any event, we are getting accustomed to sleeping in these and, compared to some of the places we have camped, the living room is like staying in a luxurious hotel.

I also think that I should get going on my Family Life badge, as well as the Genealogy badge. With those, maybe I can figure out what is happening to Grandpa. It's possible that one of our ancestors had what's happening to Grandpa happen to them, too. It sure would be nice if, through researching them, we could find some sort of cure.

As we are settling in, I run through the events of the day, and it dawns on me that I managed to go through my entire birthday without getting a single gift from my own family. Other than the balloons that Marc gave me, I didn't even get a card. I figure, with everything going on with Grandpa and moving all his stuff here, my parents didn't have time to get me a present this year. I decide that it's fine. I mean, it does say something that I went the whole day without even realizing it, so I must not care too much.

When I was younger, that never would have happened. I would have been asking about my present at breakfast. I do kind of wonder what my present would have been, though. Maybe a set of new books to explore, maybe a new phone or computer, or maybe it could have been a car. I did just turn sixteen, so stranger things have happened, right?

Now I am off on a tangent, daydreaming about different cars that I could have gotten if it was a normal birthday and our family was super rich. I could have gotten a sports car, not that it would fit my personality. I don't think I would drag race anyone in the middle of town, that's for sure. Maybe I could have gotten a truck. A lot of my friends are farmers, so they get whatever truck their family used on the farm when they turn sixteen. Then I decide I don't care at all what kind of car it could have been. I would have been elated with anything that was in good enough shape to get me from home to school and back every day.

I start writing different rhymes about cars in my poetry journal when Marc breaks my train of thought.

"What are you thinking about, Jon?"

"I just realized I didn't get a gift this year."

He quickly says, "Oh, I'm sorry. That kind of stinks."

I confess to him, "I was thinking about what it would have been like if I got a car."

Marc agrees. "Yeah, that would have been awesome. Then you could drive us anywhere we want to go."

I decide to share my last entry with him.

"If I had a car,
I know what I would do.
I would drive it around,
And take care of it, too.
It doesn't need to be much,
Just a set of four wheels.
I want a car,
So I can see how independence feels."

Marc smiles. "That's a good one, Jon."

I shrug. It's not much, and it's not like it's going to happen or anything. "Thanks. It's getting pretty late, and we have school tomorrow, so I'm going to crash. Goodnight, Marc."

"Yeah, me, too. Goodnight."

That's the end of that. My sixteenth birthday has come and gone. It turned out to be quite a day, to say the least. Full of lots of ups and downs, more so than any other day. Hopefully, tomorrow and the rest of this next year isn't as hectic as today was. I could use a little bit of calm and normalcy.

Well, nothing is going to be the same with Grandpa living here and going through whatever it is he is going through. Our family is going to have to figure out a new schedule, a new way of functioning with another person in our house. I definitely want to do my part. Otherwise, this is going to be too hard on Mom and Dad. I bet it was pretty hard for them to decide what to do with Grandpa, but I'm glad they chose to help him. I know I would do the same thing if it was them who needed my help.

Rise and Shine

Dustin

DUE TO MY COVERT MISSION last night, morning comes all too soon. My alarm starts blaring "Unskinny Bop" by Poison this morning. What I wouldn't give to have a modern, decent radio station here in Grinwell.

I wake up and immediately check on the stash of blue serum that I swiped last night. Since I know it needs to stay cool, I have it in a cooler with several ice packs to keep it as cold as possible.

I take a look and shrug. I don't even know how cold is cold enough. This is going to have to be sufficient.

Since I know for a fact that I am going to the weight room this morning, I start the day in my sweats and workout gear and put my school clothes in my bag. This will save some time and give me more of an opportunity to test what I can do with more of the blue stuff.

I take inventory of all my wrestling medals and trophies, and it all seems different now that I know more about how they were obtained. I also have a fair list of questions to ask Coach this morning. Before that, though, I am going to top off the tank.

I decide to drink all the blue stuff that I took from the freezer so I know what will happen with larger doses and also to avoid any risk of it heating up when the ice packs lose their chill. Then I head downstairs and, to my surprise, I am up and ready before Coach is today. This is unexpected and has me wondering what he is up to. He doesn't even have the coffee done yet, though it is brewing.

77

Coffee is one of those substances that smells so good but tastes so bitter that you want to immediately gag after drinking it.

I decide to start making my own protein shake, so that means one that doesn't suck.

I put in two scoops of protein, a big spoonful of peanut butter, a cup of ice, and a full banana. Finally, I am going to get to have a decent drink this morning.

Just as I start to gulp it down, Coach comes in and asks, "Exactly what are you drinking?"

I think about that for a second then go ahead and tell him.

"It's your problem if you don't have enough energy for the day," he tells me.

"Oh, I'm sure I'll be just fine, thank you."

He shakes his head. "So, do you have any questions?"

As a matter of fact, I have a ton of them, but some, I am going to answer for myself here shortly when I test this stuff out. I know I need to ask him something, though, so I start with the big one.

"What are we going to do to this special person once we find them? And how much juice can we squeeze from them?"

He seems to have expected this one. "Well, there are no set answers. We will attach them to a special machine that has been in our family for centuries, and then start it up and get what we get out of it. It hurts, for sure, but we don't kill them. We pull out what we need, and that essentially ends their ability to use their powers. It may also leave them in a weakened or compromised state up to and including permanent psychological damage. If they are not of Asgardian descent and we hook them up to this, it will kill them."

Well, that sounds unpleasant.

"So, do I have this in me, as well? And if so, are you going to try to take it from me if we don't find someone soon?"

"Yes, you do," he admits. "And to be brutally honest, I have thought of that many times. However, I would rather have you helping me so we can *both* retain and enhance our powers than take them away from you."

For now, this sounds believable to me, and I almost appreciate that he didn't lie. At least until I learn more about this and how to make this machine of ours work.

"What exactly can we do with this stuff in our systems?" I ask.

"Well, it all depends on your own genetic makeup and which of our ancestors you belong to. In our case, we get stronger, faster, and the durability of our skin is enhanced. I'm not sure if you can do anything else or not, but nobody in our line has noted any other abilities."

"I have to admit those traits have come in handy in wrestling, whether I knew I had them through this or not."

Coach continues, "I have met descendants from many other lines, including Thor's, who generally have healing powers, strength, and sometimes the ability to command lightning. Whereas the line from Freya usually has beauty, passion, fertility, and the ability to resolve conflicts peacefully. Those from her brother, Freyr, typically find wealth and other measures of success easily. Plus, they often have the ability to manipulate the weather. The worst line for descendants of Loki's to deal with is Bragi, as their feud goes way back to Asgard. They typically have the ability to control people and almost anything with a heartbeat with either music or speaking poetry, but historically, not both. Yeah, I have seen some pretty amazing things from these descendants over the years. So, at this point, it would be pretty hard for one of them to surprise me with a new ability."

"Does drinking more of it make us even stronger or is there a limit of some sort?"

He nods and concedes, "There is a limit. Drinking a little bit more makes a small difference, but mostly, it is wasteful. There is a genetic limit to what we can do."

Well, so much for that theory. I probably wasted a bit of the good stuff today, but live and learn, right?

One thing has been gnawing at me all night, and I think I know, but I want to hear it from Coach, so I ask, "So, Coach Keith ... I assume that was you?"

He doesn't beat around the bush. He nods and tells me, "Sometimes, you have to do what is required to put yourself in the position to find another Asgardian. After I was positive that a line led here, I needed a way in, and Coach Keith wasn't agreeable to vacating the spot on his own accord. So, I took matters into my own hands, literally, and then staged a little hunting expedition. It had to be done."

It looks like he actually believes that, but part of me thinks he liked ripping someone apart with his bare hands. He certainly doesn't seem to have any remorse, but it's pretty hard to tell since Coach never really shows any real emotion, except when he is angry at me. Clearly, with him, the end justifies the means.

"We can talk more about this later. We need to head to the school in a few minutes, so let me finish breakfast and a cup of coffee.

"Locke, I'm glad you know now. This will make finding someone a lot easier since I can be more direct and stop beating around the bush. Just remember that everything I do is for both of us, okay? We are in this together."

I learned quite a bit this morning. Mostly, that I need to keep an eye on Coach because, if he gets desperate enough, I am confident he will hook me up to the machine. I also learned that we don't have to kill anyone to do the extraction, which is definitely going to cause less heat, and we can still get what we want and need. I can't shake off the feeling, though, that Coach is still holding back and leaving out some key details.

I can barely wait the few minutes it takes him to finish his breakfast and coffee. I am seriously amped right now and ready to do some heavy weightlifting. I have a feeling that I am going to set personal records today, to say the least. I also have some ideas on how to see if Captain

Blue Essence

America is our target. Yep, I am really looking forward to testing how strong both of us are this morning.

81

The Corolla

Jon

I WAKE UP TO THE ALARM on my phone and have to take a few minutes to get my bearings straight. It's funny how, when you sleep in a different place than normal, it takes your mind a minute to catch up to the new surroundings. I am a bit wrapped up in the sleeping bag, too, and my initial thought, for just a split-second, is with a bit of panic, kind of like being tied up. However, I then look over and see Marc wrapped up in his own sleeping bag and immediately calm down.

Oh yeah, Grandpa is here, and so we slept in the living room, in sleeping bags.

I nudge Marc. "Hey, Marc, wake up. We have to get up and ready for school."

He moans a little and turns over the other way.

"Seriously, Marc, let's get up," I repeat, starting the process.

Reluctantly, Marc begins to follow, and we both haphazardly pick up our sleeping bags.

Why is rolling them up such a pain to do? It's funny because it seems like it should be so easy, but getting it rolled up tight enough to get it into its cloth case is always a challenge.

By the time I am done, mine kind of fits in the bag. By my estimation, even with a little bit flowing out the top, it is close enough. Marc has about the same amount of luck with his bag, but technically, they are contained, so we are good to go.

I realize getting ready is going to be a bit more of a challenge than normal. Marc brought his stuff with him, but I'm going to have to go up and grab things from my room without waking up Grandpa. Then I instantly feel bad when I remember that Grandpa most likely isn't going to know or say anything in the state that he is in.

I head upstairs and open my door a crack, taking a peek inside. And, as soon as I open it, I hear a relatively loud and frequent amount of snoring. The coast is clear.

I slide in and grab everything I need before heading to the bathroom to get changed and ready for the school day. This is a routine I am going to have to start figuring out now that I am sharing a room. It's funny how you don't think about stuff like that until you are in the situation. When I told my parents it was okay, I was only thinking, *Okay, he is sleeping in here*, but that is just the tip of the iceberg. This is going to impact my privacy in new ways that might be harder than I originally thought.

I tag team Marc, taking turns brushing our teeth and washing our hands for breakfast. It's kind of a dumb thing to do, because we are both going to have to brush our teeth again after breakfast. That's one of those morning routines that hasn't ever made sense to me.

"Breakfast!" Mom yells up the stairs.

Marc and I put everything away and head down to the kitchen.

This morning, Mom has some oatmeal ready for us. I know that doesn't sound like much, but she adds a bit of cinnamon and some other spices to make it taste amazing. It smells like a warm sweet roll, but when you eat it, there is a good balance of sweetness and flavor that makes it go down super easily.

"You know, you're lucky to get a warm breakfast every morning, right?" Marc says. "I usually have to pour myself a bowl of cereal and scrounge for milk or anything to make it wet. Heck, lots of times, I eat it dry when I am in a hurry."

I nod. "Yeah, my mom is pretty amazing, for sure."

Just a bit later, Mom and Dad come into the kitchen. Both are wearing smiles a mile wide.

I'm pretty surprised to see Dad here this late again. He is usually long gone to work by the time I come downstairs. So, once again, I know something is up. Whatever it is can't be too bad, though, since they look way too happy. I brace myself anyway. The way my luck has been going, who knows?

"Son," Dad starts, "your mom and I realized that, with all the work and excitement yesterday with moving Grandpa in, we forgot to give you your birthday gift."

"That's okay," I tell him. "I don't need anything. It was great to have all of us together last night."

"It was great," Mom says, "but we have a surprise for you."

My heart jumps a little. I absolutely love their surprises!

Then Dad holds up a key and says, "Come out to the driveway and see your new car!"

What? Oh, heck yeah, let's do this!

Marc and I both run past Mom and Dad, and I grab the key from his hand as we pass them.

We get out to the driveway, and there it is—a seven-year-old Toyota Corolla. It's a brownish-beige color, and the seats are also brown. It has a few dings and paint scrapes, but I have to say it is the most beautiful thing I have ever seen because it is mine.

Dad says, "When we moved Grandpa and Grandma's stuff, we had to decide what to do with their car, too, and since you need one, it was a pretty easy decision."

I can't stop saying, "Thank you!" I'm so excited and really want to drive it now. "Can I drive us to school?"

"Sure," Mom says with a laugh. "I have to go with, though, of course. Then, later today, I'll come and pick you up so we can go take your driving test. After you pass and get your license, then you can take it for a spin by yourself."

Wow, what an amazing way to start the day!

Bench Press

Dustin

THE RIDE TO SCHOOL with Coach is pretty quiet. We have already said more words to each other than we normally do in a day, so I'm pretty sure we have reached our max capacity on communication. Good, because I cannot stop moving my legs and fidgeting. I don't know if it's the extra blue stuff or what, but I have some serious energy to expend right now. I feel pretty amazing, like I could do about anything I wanted to right now. I like this feeling. It feels like I am about to step on the mat for the biggest wrestling match of my life, and I am so ready.

I look at Coach as he drives and start to get a little more angry at him for keeping all this to himself for so long. He has completely robbed me of being able to reach my full potential and to understand what I am even capable of. It's such a selfish move, but not surprising. Coach has always been a bit of a prick. Apparently, an extremely dangerous and even murderous prick. I should probably say something to someone about Coach Keith, but sadly, I need Coach, so I am going to have to let that one go ... for now ... and hope he wasn't dumb enough to leave any evidence behind that could potentially catch up with him.

As soon as we arrive at the school, I jump out and head straight to the locker room without even bothering to listen to what Coach has to say. I drop off my bag then head to the weight room. Once I get there, I am pleasantly surprised to find Brad is already there.

I wave at him, and he waves me over to where he is working out, warming up with some dumbbell exercises, which sounds like a fine idea.

I grab twice the weight he is using and, to my surprise, they feel as light as a feather.

I start warming up as Captain America says, "Hey, take it easy; you should probably warm up before jumping up to your max weight."

I look straight at him and say, "This is my warm-up weight."

He laughs. "Ha, right."

Well, this seems like a bit of a challenge to me. I think I'm going to have to do something about it.

I set the dumbbells down and think about the best exercise to use to test out my strength and his. Got it.

I head over to the bench press and decide it's time to see what Brad can do, as well.

"How do you feel about a little contest to see who can lift more?"

Brad lets the weights drop to the ground with a resounding *thud*. "Oh, it's on, Champ."

After we load up the bar with some forty-fives, I have to hold back. It is so easy that I think I might push the bar through the ceiling if I'm not too careful.

"C'mon, let's use some big boy weights," I egg him on. Then we throw another forty-five on each side. Now we are up to two twenty-five.

Once again, I easily rep it out and do ten of those super-fast.

He nods in approval then jumps in and does only one rep before setting it back down. "No reason to burn myself out," he excuses his wimpy attempt.

We start grabbing smaller weights, working our way up. He is now starting to struggle a little bit. You know when there is a bit of hesitation at the bottom of the lift, and you start to shake as you push it up to the top of the lift, and then it drops loudly in place on the uprights? Yep, that's him.

We finally add another forty-five to each side, so now we are up to three hundred and fifteen pounds. Then I lay back and pump out another quick ten reps. It probably looks pretty obnoxious because I'm not even pretending to be having any issues. I lay back and knock them out before popping back up and smiling the entire time. I. Feel. Unbelievable. It's like I am only lifting the bar; no weights. That's how easy it is!

Brad nods. "I'm impressed, Champ. I'm not sure I can do it."

I look at him from the bench. "It's a competition. You have to try or forfeit. What's wrong? Are you afraid of a little bit of iron?"

He grunts and flexes his muscles then gets on the bench when I stand up.

Captain America moves his hands on and off the bar, taking deep breaths, psyching himself out to make a lift attempt. Then he gets back up and walks over to get a drink of water from the drinking fountain, shaking his arms out all way back over to the bench as he slowly takes a seat and lies back into position.

I decide to give him a little bit of a lift-off so he can start with the bar up. Almost instantly, it comes crashing to his chest. I don't even bother trying to catch it as I hear a crack. I just walk out of the room, shaking my head, as Brad screams for help.

Well, I guess he's not special, either. I need to keep searching.

I think I will see who else might be here today for me to challenge.

I hear a bunch of noise coming from Brad as I create some distance between us. I'm sure it's his offensive line running over to help him out. They were surprisingly absorbed in their own lifting and talking around the water cooler, so they somehow missed all the competition until it was too late.

What a disappointment he is, but on the bright side, man, I can lift a lot of weight with the help of my little blue secret formula. It's exhilarating.

I probably should have helped Captain America, but I honestly don't care. I suppose maybe this is how Coach felt when he dealt with Mr. Keith. I have this overwhelming feeling that I did what needed to be done to test this person out. If anything, I am more disappointed than I am guilty about the whole situation. Yeah, I bet this is exactly how Coach felt killing Mr. Keith. I guess, in retrospect, that really doesn't bother me either. I'm not so different from him after all.

I head outside to get away from all the screaming, even though it's cold out, and run some laps around the track.

After two miles in under eight minutes, I realize that speed is also a side effect. I'm also not even breathing hard, so I have some serious stamina with this stuff. Because of the adrenaline and possibly the rush of excitement, I don't even really feel cold. That's interesting, as well.

I try a long jump, to see if there is anything special there, and it's like I'm literally walking on air. I easily reach twenty-four feet and am pretty sure I could do much more than that if I really let myself go. Maybe I should be a track star, too. Nah, that's not cool.

After the jump, I see Coach running out, looking pretty pissed off.

"What do you think you're doing, Locke?"

I shrug. "Testing to see what I'm capable of."

He gets more animated as he says, "This is exactly why I didn't tell you! You are behaving like a child!"

I grin back at him. "Maybe so, but you have to admit that I'm a pretty powerful child."

"You do know Brad probably has broken ribs, right? People are going to ask questions, and he already told me what you did. Which, I'm pretty sure means you somehow took more of the serum before we got here."

I look him straight in the eye and say, "So what if I did? What are you going to do about it? Nothing. That's what I thought."

"Locke," Coach warns, "I can get jacked up like this, as well, so tread lightly here. I am going to cut you a little bit of slack this time, but you *have* to keep this under control. First of all, we don't have enough for you to be blowing it on nothing; and second, people are going to get suspicious. It will hurt your chances to compete in wrestling, if that's what you want to do in college and eventually in the Olympics. You have to pace yourself."

I reluctantly nod, agreeing. "Yeah, I guess you're right." I mean, I almost feel a *little* bad about what happened. But, let's face it, I have some pretty freaking awesome powers, and the only way that will continue is if I get my hands a little dirty. I can live with that.

Driver's License

Jon

WE GET TO SCHOOL WITH me driving, Mom in the passenger seat, and Marc and Jill in the back. When we pull up to the drop-off zone, having already dropped Jill off at the middle school, we all hop out and Mom gets behind the wheel. She let Jill and Marc know that my dad would be picking them up today, so they should watch for his car. That's good, though. I would hate for either of them to have to walk home. Well, it would be kind of funny if Jill had to do that once ... maybe.

Me driving is quite a bit different than the embarrassment that happened yesterday. This time, everyone stops to check out the car, and I even get a few fist bumps as I walk toward the school entrance. Yes, this is much better. I could definitely get used to this feeling. Of course, I still have to make it through the morning before Mom picks me up early and takes me to the DMV. I have already been through driver's education, so the last thing I need to do to earn my license is to take my driving test.

As soon as we get to first period, we hear the news that there was an accident in the weight room this morning and Brad Dillon was injured.

Let me tell you, when you live in Iowa and your starting varsity quarterback is hurt, news travels fast. Really fast.

Some people say he broke some ribs and others say he broke his back. Either way, all the stories agree on who caused it.

Apparently, Dustin Locke decided to challenge Brad to a bench press contest and, well, he was significantly stronger than Brad. That's kind of shocking, really, if you look at the two of them. You have a small, one hundred and thirty pound wrestler and a star football player who probably has a good fifty pounds on him. Yeah, I would certainly say that Dustin is freakishly strong after having him whip me around on the wrestling mat yesterday. Given what happened to Brad, I now consider myself pretty lucky to have escaped that period without a major injury, though I am still sore all over.

When conversations this juicy get started, it impacts every class until the truth is finally known, or whatever lie is accepted as the truth. It also gets pretty loud and a bit rowdy. Of course, that all stops the instant Dustin walks into the room. Then it's so quiet so fast you can hear your own heartbeat.

I find myself getting a little nervous. Last time, he sat by me in English and, well, I'm not sure I want that honor again today.

Sure enough, he boots Marc out of his seat by pointing at him then to the back of the room. Being smart, Marc quickly gets up and takes his new seat. Dustin then looks around the room and sees everyone staring at him, but he only smiles as he sits down. Then, for whatever reason, he decides to start up a conversation with me.

"Too bad about what happened to Brad this morning. I thought he said he could handle three hundred and fifteen pounds, but apparently, he isn't so special after all."

I don't say anything. I mean, I have no idea what to even say to that.

He continues, "So he broke a couple of ribs? It's not as big of a deal as everyone is making it out to be. I guess, he won't overestimate his strength so readily next time."

I shrug, nod, and try to do anything to make myself not look completely terrified of this guy. I'm sure it's not working.

I have no idea how a person could witness what he did and not be a bit shaken up over it, or worried in the slightest. That's insane to me. I can also tell you that I can't get out of first period fast enough when the bell finally rings. I want no part of any more Dustin time right now. My objective is to get through these first few periods as quickly as possible then get out of here to take that driving test.

Then I think about Jess. She must be super worried right now. If I see her, I will try to comfort her as best as I can. Not in a way that says, hey, I want to take advantage of this situation. I only want to let her know that, if she needs to talk, I am here.

She must be really upset. I know I am, and I don't even like Brad. Still, he doesn't deserve what happened to him. No matter how or why it went down.

She's not in her usual places, so my guess is she is either with Brad or with the counselor or something.

I spend almost every class after English going through all the driving rules that I can remember from driver's education class to be as ready as I can be for this test.

I tell myself, when I get into the vehicle, I have to put on my seat belt, adjust the seat, adjust the mirrors, and then start the car.

I know all this seems ridiculous, but I have to pass this test so I can drive, especially now that I have my own set of wheels. Honestly, I can't even believe I am thinking that. It hasn't really even sunk in yet. I really like that phrase—"my own set of wheels."

After going over the instructions from my driver's education teacher, what seems like a thousand times in my mind, I then spend the remaining time half-paying attention to the teacher and half-staring at the hands of the clock. I know that watching the clock isn't going to make it go any faster. In fact, if I didn't know better, I would swear that it is actually going slower. This has some merit when I watch the clock actually adjust itself as the hands hesitate, move back, and then move forward again, clicking and clacking like only an old school classroom clock does.

Finally, the bell rings, and I am being called down to the office. Of course, I know I am being called down because my mom is here to pick me up. This is probably going to be the fastest I have ever walked down to the school office. In fact, I would all-out sprint if I wouldn't get in trouble for "running through the halls."

When I get to the office and see my mom there, I am so happy. I see some of the football players are there, as well, no doubt talking about what happened earlier in the day with Principal Douglas.

As I walk by the counselor's office, I catch a glimpse of Jess, too, and my heart drops for a second, but I have to leave that to the professionals for now, as I have my own situation to attend to.

This is it! This is a pretty big day in the life of any teenager, especially around here. Once I have my license, I will have the ability to drive myself to school and, really, anywhere I need to go, which actually is pretty much just school. *Ha!* Still, I could go somewhere else if I wanted to. I am looking forward to having that choice.

As I head out to the Corolla, I remember to thank Mom one more time.

"Don't thank me yet," she tells me. "You still have to pass your driving test."

I smile. "Love you, too, Mom!"

I'm Sorry

Dustin

WELL, I HAVE TO ADMIT, my decision to test Captain America was not my most brilliant idea. I have suddenly become enemy number one to what seems like the entire school. Now I have to decide if I am going to embrace this bad boy image or if I am going to try to salvage what I can of my reputation.

I also had to spend about an hour in Principal Douglas's office, staring at that giant caterpillar on his face and listening to him describe how disappointed he is that I didn't realize Brad needed help. Of course, I had to make up some sort of excuse, so I went with having to make an emergency run to the bathroom. I told him that, with so many football players in the room, I didn't think it would be an issue if Brad needed a little bit of help. I mentioned how surprised I was that none of them bothered to help him before he got hurt. Mr. Douglas and their coach should probably talk with them about teamwork some and making sure no man is left behind and that type of thing. Yeah, it was really their fault that Brad got hurt. At least, that is the story I am sticking with officially.

The reality is this place is a means to an end, and we are clearly only here to find the special person who we need in order for Coach and me to keep the edge we have. Now that I fully understand it, there is no way I am going to give this up.

So far, we have ruled out Jon and Brad, but I still have a feeling about Jess. I wonder where she might be right now. Oh, I just realized she is probably going to be a little pissed at me right now. I am going to have to do something about that.

As Mrs. Greene is gearing up for another lecture on the price of tea in China and other mind blowing things, I decide to settle in next to Mr. Ryan and see what this guy is all about.

When I walk over and introduce myself, he says, "My name is David Ryan and, as you can tell, I'm not a huge fan of school."

Okay, I feel a kindred connection with this guy as we at least share that.

"How did you pull off that pop quiz so fast?" I ask. "I know you were engrossed in a movie, so you couldn't have heard her lecture."

"Look, I don't really know you, and class is about to start, so maybe we can have this discussion some other time. I am in the middle of one of my favorite shows and would like to get back to it, if you don't mind."

I make a hand gesture to indicate *by all means; don't let me interrupt your viewing pleasure.*

Thankfully, there are no more surprise tests, and I am able to glance over Dave's shoulder to at least enjoy the on-screen action before drifting off into a nice daydream about going to the Olympics twice so I can win two gold medals and hold it over Coach's head for the rest of our lives. The daydream is just getting good, too, when the bell rings and I have to park that for a minute to continue the task at hand.

I decide to wander the halls between the rest of the classes today to see if I can find Jess, or if I, by chance, notice anyone else who might stand out. I still need to get answers from Dave. I also have to decide the best way to safely test others to see if they have any Asgardian heritage that will draw zero attention. I don't think I'm going to be able to easily explain a bunch of injuries following me around wherever I go.

Part of me wonders if this could be something some kids are just unaware of having, like I was until last night. In my case, Coach was aware and was helping me to excel by feeding me the blue serum that

I need to trigger my abilities. If he hadn't been doing that, I would not have known. It's possible that I would have been a miserable nobody like everyone else.

I suddenly remember the time that I had someone else try the blue stuff, and they thought it was disgusting. That may be something that I can work with as a costly but safe test without drawing a bunch of additional attention to myself.

Finally, after the last bell of the day rings, I see Jess. She is about to leave, so I have to jog to catch up with her.

Whoa, I guess I'm still a little juiced up since I catch up with her in an instant. I really need to be more careful with that.

As she turns around, I startle her, and she takes a quick step back.

"Sorry, Jess," I apologize. "I didn't mean to sneak up on you like that. Can we talk for a second, please?"

By the look on her face, as expected and surely warranted, she is not interested in having anything to do with me. I'm going to have to try to turn on the charm here.

"I know everyone is saying that I intentionally hurt Brad this morning, but I really didn't. He's a great guy and possibly my only friend at this school, so I am sorry about what happened to him. I really thought he said he had the weight and didn't need help. I never would have walked away to use the bathroom otherwise." I do my best to look her straight in the eye and to be as sincere as possible, and I can tell she is trying to decide whether to buy my story or not.

She shakes her head and replies, "That is not what I heard from Brad."

I continue with my apologetic tone and say, "You know how us guys are sometimes—a little stubborn and pig-headed, not wanting to admit we did something stupid. I know what both Brad and I did was dumb. I mean, who really cares which of us can lift more? That could easily have been me taking the injury. I'm such an idiot!"

She looks down and tilts her head a little then nods, indicating I am making some progress here.

"Where are you off to?" I ask.

"I am heading to go see Brad. He needs to stay in the hospital overnight, so I am going to keep him company for a bit until visiting hours are over."

I nod. "Do you mind if I come by a bit later so I can visit and tell him how sorry I am?"

She hesitates. "I don't know if that's a good idea, Dustin. It might be too soon, you know? I think you have done quite enough with him today."

I put my hands together to indicate sincerity. "Please?"

I guess you do catch more flies with honey because she finally agrees.

"Okay, come by in an hour or so, and we can ask Brad. That's the best I can do, Dustin."

"Deal. Thanks!"

Now I am going to have to find Coach and convince him of my little plan to test out Jess.

When I get to Coach's office, he is already waiting for me.

"What took you so long?"

"I was talking with Jess about Brad."

He gives me a stern look. "I'm not sure that is a good idea after this morning."

I raise up my hand to deny his protest. "It went fine. In fact, it went better than fine. I need to talk with you about meeting them at the hospital in an hour so I can apologize to Brad."

His eyes widen a little. I think I surprised him a bit.

I continue, "And I have an idea about how we can test Jess while we're doing that."

"I guess it's probably better if you don't work out tonight, anyway. So, what is your idea?"

"I want to bring some food and drinks to the hospital for Brad and Jess. I can tell them that I figured they could use some good food after the day they had and as a means to show that I want to make amends."

He motions for me to keep going and get to the point.

"I figure I can get some fast food with blue sports drinks in the combo meals. I then want to slip some of the blue stuff into the drink."

"What?" he protests. "We are already super low on it! Why would we do that?"

"Remember what happened when I gave Rodney a taste that one time and you freaked out?"

He nods.

"Well, he thought it was disgusting, so I'm pretty sure all humans feel that way, right?"

He thinks for a minute then grins. "I like it. Let's do it."

The Driver

Jon

WHEN WE GET TO OUR local DMV, I really start to sweat. I have all the symptoms of a serious case of the nerves—butterflies in my stomach, sweaty hands, and I am fidgeting like a mouse on caffeine running through a maze. I fumble with everything as I give the unimpressed lady at the desk my birth certificate, social security card, and everything else we brought with us, which is probably overkill, but hey, as Mom says, better to bring too much than too little. At this moment, however, all I can do is drop it all on the lady's counter.

She is the type of person who you can tell hates her job but does it because she has to. Either that or she has used up all her smiles for the day. She hands us some paperwork with a look of indifference and tells us to have a seat, fill it out, and bring it back when we are finished.

Once we are done with that, we get a number and now wait with the rest of the people for one of the few test administrators to become available. This is one of those things that always seems to take forever. But, in this case, it actually does take a long time.

After we have waited for over an hour, Mom starts to get a little impatient and goes up to the lady to ask if she knows how much longer it will be.

I can tell this lady hears this all the time because she says, "Ma'am, I have no idea. Just be patient and, eventually, your number will be called."

Mom sits back down, clearly not happy with that answer, but both of us shrug because there isn't a thing we can do about it.

To help kill time and to take Mom's mind off the wait, I decide to talk to her some about the requirements of the Genealogy badge that I am pursuing for Boy Scouts.

"Mom, I started working on my Genealogy badge, and I really want to build out our family tree as far back as possible. I have this idea that, if I go back far enough, maybe we will find someone who has had a similar medical condition as Grandpa. Then we can see if it was diagnosed or if they somehow recovered on their own."

"Oh, Jon, that's a fantastic idea!" Mom replies. "When we were packing up Grandma and Grandpa's things, I am pretty sure he had a pretty extensive book that traced their side of the family back for hundreds of years. If we had more time to look at it, I definitely would have, but the move was so rushed that I had to throw it in a box and move on. When we get back to the house, I can help you find it in the garage. I'm sure Grandpa would love for you to take a look. It's so sweet of you to think of that. I also appreciate you taking my mind off this long wait, as well. I was starting to get a little frustrated with our friend at the desk."

I smile. "I know, Mom. I'm sure it won't be much longer. And I would love to see Grandpa's family tree and any other books that he might have stashed away that could help me learn about our family. Thank you."

We sit quietly for what seems like another hour but is really only fifteen minutes when my number finally gets called and I jump up.

Mom is super excited, giving me a hug and telling me, "Good luck. Go get 'em, Tiger."

I smile as I head toward the door where a large old man is waiting to go for a ride with me.

When we step outside, I approach the car and decide that I'm going to check the exterior and look like I know what I'm doing by kicking the tires, etc. I then get into the car and run through the steps that I have been practicing in my mind all day—seat belt, adjust seat, adjust mirror, foot on the brake, and then I start the car. My hands are positioned at ten and two as I look over to the elderly man in the passenger seat.

"What are you waiting for?" he asks. "You may begin."

I make several turns and always use my turn signal, constantly checking my speed to make sure it is correct and glancing around at all the mirrors. Basically, I do my best impression of Dad driving, without yelling at all the other drivers for being stupid. Then I attempt parallel parking, but I don't quite get close enough to the curb, which causes my copilot to scribble a bit on his notepad. We finally make our way back to the DMV, and I pull into the parking spot where the drive started.

The man has already spent a few minutes tallying everything. I swear he is counting using his fingers and toes.

I start to get worried. What could there be to actually count other than mistakes?

Finally, he puts the notepad down and declares, "Congratulations, you passed!"

Those are the absolute *best* words anyone has ever spoken to me! Is it wrong for me to want to give this guy a hug? Probably. Instead, I smile the goofiest smile ever and shake his hand. "Thank you, sir, thank you so much!"

"That never gets old. Congrats, kid!" He chuckles and goes back inside to get his next assignment. He is clearly less moved by this experience than I am yet satisfied that he has done his job.

I head back inside and tell Mom, who gives me a big old hug and tells me how proud she is. Then the lady behind the desk clears her throat and says, "Let's get a quick picture for your license."

When I give the geekiest smile ever, standing before the camera, the lady says, "No smiles."

I do my best to contain it for a minute, and then she prints out my temporary license and hands it to me.

If I'm honest, it is a bit of a letdown. I was really hoping for my permanent license, but I will get over it. All that matters is I can drive now, on my own. I can't believe it! This is going to be so great!

I quickly head out the door before they change their mind, walking past all the other people who are tired of waiting for their turn. I'm a little sad for them. Mostly, I just want to get in the car and drive. So, I do that, taking us home.

Pulling into the driveway, I ask Mom, "Can I go pick up Marc so we can drive around a bit before dinner?"

"Yes. Have fun and make good choices."

I act like I hate it when she says that. Secretly, it makes me happy to know she cares. I give her a hug, and then I drive off.

When I get to Marc's house, I realize that I forgot to text him. *Duh!* So, I shoot him a quick message.

I passed. I am outside your house right now in the Corolla.

I add a smiley face, and before I can type another word, he is running out the front door. From the look on his face, I'm not sure which of us is more excited.

"Congrats!" Marc cheers. "I knew you'd do it!"

I tell him all about the DMV, the guy administering the test, and how he made me wait while he tallied my score.

"Sounds rough," Marc says. "But all that matters is you are legal now! Let's go!"

We start driving around.

"Let's scoop the loop!" Marc suggests.

"Really? I mean, that's so lame, right?"

He gives me that do-it-for-me look, and I relent.

"Okay, why not?"

When it gets close to dinnertime, knowing Dad is going to want to have some words with me, I head back to drop off Marc, telling him, "I'll pick you up for school tomorrow."

"Don't be late!"

I head home where Dad is waiting for me in the driveway with his phone in his hand. He has clearly been tracking me, which is ironic since that is something I do whenever I wait for him or Mom to pick me up from somewhere. Those occasions should be few and far between now.

"Tracking me?" I ask. "How did I do?"

He smiles. "Just fine, son. I see kids still scoop the loop, after all. Congrats on getting your license!" He gives me a high-five. Dad is the one person left on earth who still does that. "You got back just in time to eat with all of us." Then he gives me a big hug before we head inside to eat. I soak up the moment and can't help but feel a little bit taller and a lot more like a man than a boy. It feels good.

After dinner, I go back outside with a bunch of cleaning supplies. I wash the car off as best I can, but it's really, really cold and turns out to be not such a good idea in Iowa in the middle of winter. So, then I focus on wiping down the inside of the car and turning the stale smell that overwhelms your nose into something that's a mixture of stale and clean. I keep the car running, listening to the radio, and then I stay in the car until bedtime, enjoying the fact that I have a car. I actually have my own car. This is a total game changer. I cannot wait to write about this in my poetry journal and drive myself to school in the morning! Best. Day. Ever!

Class Clown

Dustin

I AM PRETTY RELIEVED that Coach is going along with my plan. We head home first to get a small amount of the blue serum, and then we head through the drive-thru of the only fast food burger joint in this town before heading to the hospital. Fortunately, they offer a blue sports drink that is going to be perfect to conceal our supplement.

As we pull up to the hospital, Coach says, "Okay, so I am going to do my best to try to support you, so follow my lead when we get in there."

I nod while thinking to myself that I will do whatever I think I need to do in the moment to get them to drink this stuff. I open the lids and slip it into their drinks.

As soon as we walk into the room that Captain America is staying in, his eyes land right on me and lock on.

"Dillon," Coach starts, "we thought both of you might enjoy a bite to eat from the outside."

Captain America stops him and growls while pointing directly at me, *"What are you doing here, mullet head?"*

Coach starts to talk, but I interrupt him. "I'm sorry, Brad. The competition got the best of us—the best of me. I should have been there to spot you. I'm really sorry. I was telling Jess that your friendship means a lot to me, and I didn't mean to blow it."

"But you walked away right after the lift-off," Brad insists. "That's so not cool."

I nod in agreement. "I know. No excuses here. I'm man enough to admit when I make a mistake. How about you?"

I can already tell Captain America respects that. He is still rightfully upset, but a man to man apology has to be at least acknowledged.

"I get it," he says. "But don't expect me to lift like that with you ever again."

I hold my hands up. "Hey, I don't blame you one bit."

Jess grabs the food and drinks, saying, "Thank you. The hospital cafeteria is pretty bad here."

They both grab a few French fries and pop them into their mouths. They are good and salty, so it shouldn't take too many to get this show on the road. To my surprise, however, they both get through all their fries before reaching for their drinks. Jess drinks, and then Brad, and almost at the same time, both their faces scrunch up.

"Ugh," Jess says. "I think there is something wrong with the syrup for this sports drink. It tastes so bad. How is yours, Brad?"

"It is pretty rancid, honestly."

She takes his from him and walks over to the sink, dumping them both out. With that, our hopes of them being special go down the drain with the blue sports drink laced with blue serum.

Well, there is no point sticking around here anymore. Coach and I need to go back to the drawing board and see if we can figure out who else we might want to test for special abilities. This drink test was fine once, but now I am regretting wasting even a drop of the blue stuff, so I don't think I'm going to be inclined to want to try that again.

I look at Captain America then at Jess. "If you will excuse us, Coach and I need to get back to the house for dinner and so he can plan his torture—I mean, drills—for tomorrow. I hope you feel better soon, Brad."

"Thank you, man," Captain America says. "And thanks for the food. Even if the drink was horrible, the fries hit the spot. I'll see you at school, Champ."

Better than mullet head, I tell myself as I smile then head out the door to continue the search.

When we get out into the parking lot, Coach parrots what I was already thinking. "Well, neither of them are what we are looking for, and I don't think we want to waste any more of our supply on a taste test, Locke."

I nod. "Agreed on both points, Coach. I'm really disappointed, because I thought it was going to be one of those two."

As soon as we get home, we make a quick dinner, and then I head straight to where Coach keeps all his research to try my best at identifying anyone who might stand out from the crowd at school for literally any reason. I'm so focused on the research that it runs well into the night, and I wake up to find my head on a hard surface.

As I open my eyes, I see I am still sitting in the chair with my head on the table. I peel my head up and find a picture stuck to my forehead, dangling down into my eyes. It's a picture of Marc Miller, aka Thor. I think about it for a minute then realize that big things can come in small packages, and it's possible that his interest in Thor comes from something deeper than watching a movie or reading a book. I'm not sure why it took me this long to put it together once I found out all this actually exists. We have gym class together, so I might be able to test him like I did Bragg the other day.

I have to hurry to get ready. I also realize this means I haven't done any of my homework. *Crap.* But compared to this work, that really doesn't matter right now.

I choke down yet another protein shake. Then, as Coach and I head to the school, I let him in on the plan.

"I think I would like to challenge Marc Miller in class today. I don't know why I overlooked this, but everyone calls him Thor. I thought it was because he was dorky and always has Thor shirts on and has a kids' Thor backpack."

"I doubt there is anything special there," Coach replies. "I have been around a lot of Asgardians, and he falls short on potential. Then again, it doesn't hurt to test him out with wrestling and see what happens."

So, it is agreed; we will test Marc Miller next.

At school, I immediately head to the locker room and am met with the realization that nobody wants to work out with me because of the whole "Brad incident." Whatever. That makes sense. Of course, I also threw the entire offensive line under the bus with Principal Douglas, so I am now both a jerk and a snitch. Not popular qualities for an athlete in the weight room.

I end up doing my own lifting while planning how I am going to test out "Thor" when I get the chance later in the day. We are going to need to put him in a situation where he has to show a quick jolt of speed or strength to get away from me. Yeah, so that is pretty much any escape or move.

As I mindlessly do calf raises, I tell myself to not overthink this. I will pair up with Thor and do what I do best—wrestle.

While squatting a pretty heavy weight, one of the football players comes up behind me and tries to kick out one of my legs. I simply drop the weight and turn around to glare at him. However, before I get in any more trouble, I say, "Sorry, I didn't know you wanted the squat bar that badly. I'll see you later." Then I walk off and hit the showers.

I can't let someone bait me into a fight right now. Then I would have to explain how I could smash his face in, and I don't have time for that right now or enough credit with the principal to get any more leeway. The last thing I need is to get myself suspended for conduct and risk the wrath of the "no tolerance policy" on violence that was batted around in our last little chat in his office.

When I get to my first period English class, I see Bragg and Thor are in their usual spots. It looks like Thor hasn't learned his new place is in the back of the room. Then again, this works for today's agenda.

Instead of pointing at Thor, I point at Bragg, telling him to get to the back so I can sit by Thor. He complies, of course, because, well, he already knows he is no match for me after wrestling me the other day.

As Mr. Young gets started, he says, "I hope everyone did their homework from yesterday, as I am going to have you present your answers before the class."

Everyone moans in unison, and I start to sweat a little, having no idea what we were supposed to do. I hope I can piece it together from whatever the people before me say.

Just then, my luck runs out as Mr. Young says, "Mr. Locke, front and center."

Of course I am going first. What a way to start the day.

His first question for me is, "What is the source of the conflict between the Montagues and Capulets?"

I don't have any idea, to be honest, so I say, "I guess it's because of Romeo and Juliet."

"How so?" Mr. Young asks.

"Well, he likes her and she likes him, and neither family likes that."

"This isn't social media, Mr. Locke," Mr. Young says, "where everyone is consumed by likes and shares. Nice try, but F."

The whole class starts laughing at me as I take my seat.

I look next to me and see Thor with a smile on his face and take a mental note of that as I glare at him.

On the Spot

Jon

THIS MORNING, I WOKE up to a beautiful winter day. It was frigid for sure, but none of that mattered as I jumped out a bed with an extra hop in my step.

All I could think was that today will be the first time I drive myself to school without a parental unit by my side!

That's right. Prepare to be dazzled by my bright shiny teeth that I just brushed as I pull into the parking lot. There isn't anything that is going to put a damper on my day.

I head downstairs, but there is no breakfast made. I am super early and probably overly eager to hit the road. No worries. I make myself a bowl of cereal and, like everything else, it tastes amazing today.

As I am finishing the first bowl, Mom comes walking into the kitchen. "Oh, Jon, you startled me. I didn't expect you to be up so early."

"I'm pumped to drive us to school today." I grin.

"Ha, I understand. Jon-boy, can you take Jill to school, as well, this morning and every other morning from now on?"

I can tell she is pretty happy about this and the extra time she is going to have every morning. Knowing I am the cause of this, I proudly say, "Of course, I would be happy to do that, Mom." But then it dawns on me that now I'm going to have to wait for Jill, who takes her own sweet time.

"I'm going out to warm up the car," I tell Mom. "Let Jill know to come out as soon as she is ready to go." Then I add on the way out the door, "Oh, and tell her to hurry up because the bus leaves in twenty minutes."

Mom chuckles but mutters under her breath, "Good luck with that."

I grab my stuff and head out to the car to start it up, scraping off the windows then sitting there, listening to music. About thirty minutes later, Jill comes walking out, and she doesn't like it much when I stick my hand out and point for her to get in the back seat.

She mockingly gets in, saying, "Chauffeur, please take me to school. Chop! Chop!"

"Hardy, har, har. You're so funny."

Mom comes running out, waving her arms, and then she takes about three dozen pictures before I can finally pull out of the driveway.

Just like yesterday, when we get to Marc's house, he is already outside, ready to go.

He looks in and grins as he realizes he is in the front seat, as well. "Nice, I could get used to this."

"Well, go right ahead," I reply.

"The car looks great and smells better. Did you work on it all night or did you get your homework done?" he asks.

I drop my head. "Man, I forgot to do my homework." I start to panic. "I have never done that before. What am I going to do?"

Jill laughs. "Ha, you are going to be in so much trouble when Mom and Dad find out. They will probably take the car away."

I look in the mirror and warn her, "Not a word of this gets back to Mom and Dad, understand? We need to establish a safe zone here in the car. Whatever you hear in the car is not to be repeated, and we will do the same for you."

She smiles and says, "What's it worth to you?"

Great, extortion. I will deal with this after school, or not. She isn't going to be a pushover, that much is clear.

After dropping her off and getting closer to school, my heart starts racing a bit. I am in a jam now. I'm not really paying attention to whether anyone watches me pull in, and I think they might be trying to talk to me, but I am focused on heading straight to English class with Marc.

When we get there, I ask if I can look at his homework real quickly. I have only read a couple of things when Dustin walks in and heads straight for us. Marc starts to get up, but this time, Dustin points to me then to the back of the class.

Huh? Okay, I guess that means *I* get to move today.

I hand Marc his homework then take my new place in the back of the class, wondering what Dustin is up to.

When Mr. Young gets in, he says we are going to have an oral exam on our homework from last night. Yep, now I am starting to feel a little queasy. This is not good. I am not prepared, and Mr. Young is one of my favorite teachers. If I disappoint him, I'm not sure how I will ever be able to look him in the eyes again.

Fortunately, he calls on Dustin first, and when he reluctantly walks up, I start to think he may be in the same boat as I am.

Mr. Young asks him about why the Montagues and Capulets were feuding. What? I don't know that answer myself. I start to jot down something while Dustin completely fumbles his way through an answer, saying "like" a lot of times. I'm still pretty focused when I hear the whole class laugh, so I start laughing, too, guessing something was funny. However, as I look up, Dustin is glaring at everyone, including me, and then he is focused on Marc for an awkward amount of time, staring angrily.

"Mr. Bragg, front and center," Mr. Young says. "Educate Mr. Locke on what the answer is to that question."

Oh man, no way.

I somehow manage to put one foot in front of the other as I march my way up to the front of the class, tightly holding onto the piece of paper that I ripped from my notepad.

"Go ahead, Mr. Bragg," Mr. Young encourages.

I look down at my piece of paper and read it without looking up.

> *"The answer is: I do not know,*
> *Any more than I expected this test.*
> *The feud had gone on for years and years,*
> *but sadly, like everyone else,*
> *I know not the rest."*

There is silence. Everyone is shocked by what I said.

Mr. Young looks up then down and pauses for an eternity before he says, "Exactly, Mr. Bragg! Nobody knows the reason why the two families were fighting. Good job. A."

I head back to my seat, walking past a fuming Dustin, while Marc has the widest eyes ever. He sticks out his fist for me to knock it as I walk by.

I mean, you have to do that and not leave a friend hanging, so I give him a fist bump back then take my seat.

That was a close call. Now I start to worry about all my other classes today that I am not prepared for. This is going to be a challenging day.

Class Dismissed

Dustin

THE BELL SOUNDS, INDICATING this hour of hell is over and I can get out of here. I make my way out to the hallway but decide to wait to have a little conversation with the two nerds.

As I see Marc and Jon walk out of the classroom, I make my way over and look Marc directly in the eyes. "So, you thought it was funny watching me get an F, did you?"

He shakes his head. "I didn't think it was funny. I just laugh when I get really nervous. See?" He laughs a little, but it's certainly less convincing than it was earlier.

"That's not an excuse, *Thor*," I snip back, making sure to emphasize the use of the name to see if I get a reaction, but there is nothing new, just a healthy amount of fear.

I turn to Bragg next. "Nice poem. I mean, you got pretty lucky there, don't you think?"

"I don't know was a legitimate answer," he says. "And I think I am sticking with it now, as well."

"Well," I start, "I know you didn't know that I didn't know was what you needed to know."

"What?" Jon asks.

I slam my hand into the locker beside his head as hard as I possibly can. Then I turn my attention back to Thor, not really caring that Bragg is calling me out for whatever scrambled words I said.

I decide to elaborate on what I am going to do by saying, "Thor, I am going to partner up with *you* for wrestling drills today. If you

113

thought what I did to your girlfriend here was bad, just wait until everyone sees what I do to you. I am going to break you in half. We will see who is laughing then." I press my finger into his chest and push him back into the lockers behind them.

"I'm sorry. I didn't mean to upset you."

I am already walking away before he finishes whatever pointless plea he is trying to make, but from over my shoulder, I say, "See you after lunch."

In the next class, I end up thinking more about what I might be able to eventually do if I can collect the essence of enough of the other Asgardian descendants. It strikes me that it is also really important for my line to be the only line that exists. If Coach and I can manage to take out every other Asgardian line, it will make it better for us and for every Loki that comes after me. It also means I definitely need to make sure to have a kid to ensure we have an heir to our heritage.

If Coach becomes a problem, I can eventually end him. He hasn't really been much of a father anyway. But first things first, I need to learn more about how everything works.

There has to be a faster way to find an Asgardian. I get why Coach is studying genealogy, but there must be websites and companies that can speed this along. I remember reading about organizations that exist to help you understand your genetics better and where you come from. I have no idea how that works exactly, but I think that is exactly the type of thing that we need. If we could get enough samples, and if we could isolate whatever it is that makes an Asgardian different, then we could have our pick of which ones we want to take out and drain. I think Coach has been thinking too small and has been taking them one at a time. We need a bigger plan, one that is more of a comprehensive net so we can overthrow the world.

Wait a minute. That won't work either.

I don't know what I'm thinking. If we eliminate every other Asgardian line, then we will no longer have a source of the blue serum.

So, what we need to do is figure out exactly what it is and either try to replicate it or we will need a farm of Asgardians that are under our rule that we can mine from all the blue essence we need or want. Yes, that definitely is the answer. Anything else would likely lead to the end of my line, along with the total extinction of the Asgardian people. That is not the answer if it includes us dying out, so we are going to have to think of a smarter plan to allow us to have a steady stream of blue serum coming in. Then we will never run out of it and always know where more is coming from next.

As I'm mulling over Asgardians and world domination between my next class, I run into Jess and see that she is somewhat back to normal. She seems less offended by my existence, which is probably a good thing. I ask her how Brad is doing, and she says he passed all the additional tests and should be coming home today.

I guess it will be a while before he is back in school, though, but as soon as he is feeling better, the restrictions will ease up more and more until he is back to normal activities in a few weeks, or a couple of months, tops.

I tell her, "Thank you for the update!" I really do hope he heals up quickly so he can help me find someone special and/or at least cover up for the mistake that I made. I should have thought of another way to test him, that's for sure. Sometimes it is just too easy to get caught up in having this power. I see that now.

I head off to my next class and echo back to her, "Tell Brad hello for me whenever you see him next, and that we miss having him around."

She nods in acknowledgement with a little smile, which definitely means I am back in her good graces.

Early Dismissal

Jon

MARC AND I NARROWLY escape a confrontation with Dustin. I know everyone laughed at him in class, but at least, in my case, I completely understand the feeling. That could have easily been me, as I, too, was completely unprepared and honestly had no idea that "I don't know" was the right answer. I literally did not know.

Dustin clearly caught on to that, so I can understand why he was lashing out a bit that he had to be the butt of the joke when I clearly deserved to absorb some of it, as well. I am not going to forget this feeling.

I am definitely still excited about the car, but I cannot let that interfere with the rest of my life. For me, my best chance to move forward in life is through getting good grades so I can earn some scholarships and get into a great college. I cannot afford to get caught up in the here and now at the expense of my future.

Marc snaps me out of it when he punches me in the shoulder.

I have no idea why he does that. He knows I absolutely hate it.

"What?"

Marc excitedly says, "Jon, what happened in English was crazy! That's the second time!"

I have to ask, "The second time for what? I have never bailed on my homework before."

"No, that's the second time you said a poem and it came true. The first time was when you got the car, and now you said a poem when you were totally winging it in class, and you somehow got an A from Mr. Young! I think we may be on to something here."

"Oh, the poem ... right."

He carries on, "Jon, I'm serious. I think we should test this out."

Well, this should be interesting.

"What would you like me to test it on, Marc?" I ask only to entertain the guy. I don't really believe in what he is insinuating.

"I can't face Dustin in gym class," Marc quickly responds, "so whatever it is, it has to involve canceling school or, at a minimum, that class."

"Well, I don't think I can conjure up a snow day and early dismissal," I joke.

He apparently doesn't hear the negative in that. He nods in approval. "That's brilliant. Definitely do that!"

I laugh at him and shake my head as I start walking down the hallway.

Marc has to jog a little to catch up with me. At this point, he sounds desperate and is to the point of begging when he says, "Jon, please. Can't you just give it a try? What is the worst that could happen?"

I laugh. "Okay, okay." I have to think about this for a minute, and then I say,

"On this day,
We find we need to go.
So please cancel school,
Due to a large amount of snow".

Then I clap my hands together and rub them up and down to indicate I am finished.

Marc seems satisfied. "Thank you!" he practically praises.

I keep walking, shaking my head. You have to love this guy's persistence and total willingness to be open to anything, even the impossible. Maybe he should use that creative thinking to figure out a way to deal with Dustin himself.

Oddly enough, during our next period, it actually does start to snow.

Marc is in this class with me, as well, and he is pointing outside now pretty much nonstop.

Here's the thing, though. This is Iowa, and it's winter, so the chances of it snowing any day are pretty high. Plus, these are light flurries, so it's unlikely that anything will come from it.

Just as I start to think that way, though, and start to feel more and more confident about it, the snow picks up significantly.

You would think this is a sight that Marc has never seen before. He is now pointing in every direction like a traffic cop, making sure everyone sees and acknowledges his signals.

When this class is dismissed and we exit to the hallway, the snow is all that Marc can talk about.

"It's happening, Jon! It is going to come true. I know it."

I shrug. "It's winter; snow happens."

We start heading to our next classes when we hear the familiar *pop* right before an announcement is made. Then we hear over the loud speaker, "*Attention students: due to the snow storm that is heading our way, we are starting the early dismissal process. School will let out at noon, so make sure you are ready to safely get home at that time.*"

Of course there is a loud cheer throughout the halls. This is critical for two reasons. The first is we all love a good snow day, and the second is, since we are making it to lunch, this won't cause a makeup day, so this is literally the best-case scenario.

Of course, this also sends Marc into literal overdrive.

"Dude, you totally have a superpower! This is awesome! What are you going to do with it next?"

I look him straight in the eye and say, "Maybe I'll wish for a friend who isn't clinically certifiable."

This doesn't faze him in the slightest.

"All superheroes doubt their powers at first. What you're feeling is totally normal."

I shake my head. "You are only out of your mind excited because you don't have to face Dustin today in gym class."

He nods. "Yep, I am most definitely excited and grateful to you. For the record, I am going to be your sidekick, right?"

"What?"

"Every superhero needs a human sidekick," he explains, "and I better be yours!"

I am ready to agree to anything to get this to stop, so I say, "Sure, Marc, you can be my sidekick."

He double pumps one arm to indicate how excited he is to have this high honor.

I'm still not convinced, so I shake my head again. But, as long as he is happy, what is the harm? Then again, it is a pretty strange coincidence that now, for the third time, my poems have seemed to come true. I need some time to process this and come up with a logical explanation. I'm sure there has to be one.

What Are You Doing?

Dustin

I CANNOT EVEN BEGIN to describe how disappointed I am that we have early dismissal due to snow. I really wanted to test out Thor in hopes of getting lucky and hitting the jackpot with him so our search could be over. Instead, now I am going to have to sit around here, at this stupid school, and wait for Coach to make sure that everyone is gone and that the school is "prepared" for the snow storm. Whatever that means.

What is there to prepare for exactly? The snow fences have been up all winter and, other than fresh snow, nothing is particularly new. I suppose maybe they throw sand down in places or something. Who knows?

As I am packing up my homework at my locker, I see David making his way toward the exit and call out to him, "Hey, Dave, hold up!" This is one potential candidate I can deal with today.

He turns around then gives a look like he doesn't want to be bothered, and I would know since I pretty much invented that look.

I wonder if this guy is super smart or exactly how he can just blow off class entirely and still ace tests. To me, that seems pretty special. I have to struggle to pay attention, and I don't get anywhere near the grades this guy gets. Maybe he has some super Asgardian intelligence or something going for him. Who knows?

Seeing as he is in an apparent hurry, I cut right to the chase and ask, "How is it that you are able to do so well in Algebra when all you do is watch movies all class?"

He looks one way then the other before he says, "Look, I'll let you in on a little secret, but if you say anything, I will totally deny it."

Hm, maybe we are getting somewhere.

I nod. "Sure. I gotta know, so let me have it."

"So, I am the youngest of six kids, and all of them have gone to GHS, and all of them have had Mrs. Greene. She recycles all the homework and quizzes every year since she has been here for, like, a million years," he explains. "So, I basically have the answers to everything and memorize them before coming to school."

I take in this confession and realize the genius of it. However, that means he isn't special; he is sufficiently street smart.

"I like it." I nod. "I like it a lot. I guess that's at least one advantage to having a big family and being the youngest." I wouldn't know what that's like since it's just me in our family. I haven't thought of that advantage before. I'm sure this isn't the only class that it helps him with either. I would probably never write a paper. I would pick one of the one's that one of my older siblings wrote and touch it up a little. Yeah, that's interesting, but not the type of special that I am looking for ...

He shrugs with a grin then waves and is on his way out the door.

I like that guy, but we can cross David off our list, as well. However, if I continue to struggle in Algebra, I may have to get in on his legacy homework scheme.

Turning around, I decide to head to the wrestling room to see if anyone is there so I can run some drills. To my surprise, quite a few guys are taking this as an opportunity to get in some more practice. I see Big John Stone, who is our heaviest wrestler and a mountain of a man, and his brother, Jason Stone, who is like a mini version of him. They are doing foot speed and sprawling drills right now.

I figure I might as well change and work with these two; possibly even put them to the test, as well, since they are here.

I work with Jason first since we are closer in weight. We do foot work drills that show he is pretty quick, so this could be interesting. We tie up, and he goes for a snap down. I drop to both knees instantly and go into a double leg takedown. Too easy.

We keep going for a bit, but I am throwing him around with ease and quickly pinning him, so there isn't too much to see.

Since these guys are brothers and they think they are pretty funny, in between drills, they decide to tag team on me. Jason runs over and tags Big John, who comes barreling at me. I easily toss him.

For a big guy, John is surprisingly weak, and like lots of big guys, he is considerably slower. Therefore, I am able to make short work of him and easily pin him several times. Now, I'm pretty sure that is the blue stuff kicking in, since there is no real reason I should be able to throw him around like a paper weight.

This goes on for about an hour with few breaks. Both of them are seriously winded by the time Coach walks into the room and says, "Hey, what are you girls doing in here? School has been dismissed. You need to get home *now*!"

They both protest while I look at Coach and shake my head. I am so sick of him using that "girls" line. It's so unnecessary. And it bothers me more that he gets the satisfaction of knowing he got under my skin *again*.

"Coach, we were just wearing Dustin down."

He looks at them, seeing they are dripping with sweat, and then he looks over at me, who is as fresh as the minute I walked in. "Yeah, I see that," he says. "Maybe next time you will have better luck, guys. now get on home."

"Yes, sir!" they both say.

As soon as they walk out of the room, Coach starts up. "Locke, what exactly do you think you are doing?"

"I was testing them, Coach. We talked about testing all the wrestlers, remember?"

He shakes his head, as if I didn't hear him correctly. "In English class. I'm talking about English, genius. Mr. Young came to talk to me and said you aren't doing your homework, that you aren't taking the class seriously, and you got an F today."

I look away, as if I am bored. Frankly, I already know all of this, so none of it is news to me. The only thing annoying is that stupid Mr. Young had to go and blab to Coach about me. What a jerk!

Coach raises his voice a notch, asking, "Well, what do you have to say for yourself?"

I snip right back, "Look, Coach, I don't care about English, and I don't care about this stupid school. I only care about finding what we are after. So, you can bust my balls over this, or we can get back to more important things."

Coach doesn't think much of that answer and immediately responds with, "Your ancestors would be disgusted by how little you care about your reputation and how you are carrying yourself. You will not fail *anything* again, and you will be doing some extra credit tonight to turn that F into a C, got it?"

I nod. I don't see the point in fighting this, as he clearly thinks he has it all worked out.

In general, I know that he cannot be reasoned with when he is like this, so I am going to go into full-on ignore mode now.

I head to the locker room to get changed, and by the time I get back, Coach is gone. I'm sure he is in his office or he may have left me here again. Yeah, he is in his office. I see his big, balding head poking over the top of the back of his chair that is turned away from me.

When I get there, I ask, "Don't you even want to know if I think there is anything special about the Stone brothers?"

"Nah, I traced their heritage and ruled them out a while ago. I know for a fact there is no Asgardian blood left in their family line."

I constantly forget that this isn't his first rodeo, that he has been doing this for years. I definitely need to be more careful and not overlook his knowledge and experience. For now, I guess I need him. Plus, I still don't even know how to extract anything from an Asgardian if and when I do find one. I hate the fact that I am dependent on him for so much. He is such a prick and never even bothers to hear both sides of a story; he jumps to conclusions every time a situation arises. It's getting old.

Don't Be Stupid

Jon

MEETING MARC AT THE Corolla, I hurry out so I can brush the snow off the car and let it warm up. It's funny how I barely even feel the cold as I scrape the windshield and get ready to drive. It's such a great feeling to have a car that I don't care about a little bit of work to get it ready to go.

This is now one of those snows where you start at the front of the car and, by the time you get to the back, the front has snow on it again. So, I am just going to have to rely on the wipers, I guess.

I see Jess walking out to get picked up by her mom, who pulls up in their BMW SUV. Then Jess stops and seems to be looking in my direction. Weird.

Her mom glances over in my direction, too, to see who Jess is looking at, probably expecting someone else, and then she turns back to Jess, trying to get her attention, probably to tell her to get in the car and stop letting the snow inside the BMW.

Jess smiles and waves at me. "Nice car, Jon!"

"Thank you!" I quickly yell back, but she is already in the car and her mom is pulling out of the pickup zone.

Just then, I hear a noise and turn as Marc clears his throat. I didn't even see or hear him walk up. Then again, there was Jess.

"You know, if she knew you had superpowers, she might be interested."

I grab a handful of snow and throw it at his head. He ducks under the side of the car and narrowly misses the stinging sensation of ice-cold

125

snow hitting him in the face. Although, he definitely deserves it for remarks like that.

I motion for him to get in, and then we both slide into our seats and I start to pull out of the lot.

I have never actually driven in the snow by myself, so I am sliding around fairly wide, almost like I am trying to do a donut or something. After a few fish tails, I settle in, now having a feel for how much gas I can give the Corolla to keep it going in a straight line.

As we head over to the middle school to pick up Jill, of course Marc wants to talk about the developments of the day.

"Okay, so, I think we can both agree that you have some sort of power going on right now. I don't know if it's permanent or not, but you should definitely make the best of it."

We pull up to the pickup line and, as Jill hops into the back seat, I try to quiet Marc by saying, "*Shh ...*"

Well, that was clearly a mistake, because now I actually have Jill's attention, which is the exact opposite of what I wanted.

"What are the two of you talking about?" she asks.

Before I can stop him, Marc says, "We are talking about Jon's superpowers. He can make things happen by just saying a poem."

Jill, of course, thinks this is hilarious and cannot stop laughing. When she finally catches her breath, she says, "And what makes you think that exactly, Thor?"

Oh boy, here we go.

"Do you remember the night of Jon's birthday when I stayed over?" She nods.

"So, Jon wrote a poem about getting a car. I don't remember it exactly how it went, but the next day ... *boom!* he got a car. Then he spent so much time cleaning the car last night after he got his license that he forgot to do his homework and we had a quiz over it. Jon got up and said a poem ... *boom!* he got an A. Then finally, I was afraid of getting destroyed by a bully in gym class, so I asked him to conjure up a snow storm and early dismissal—"

"And *boom!*" Jill interrupts.

Marc nods, thinking she finally understands, but I know better. That is not how my sister thinks.

She starts out strong. "Thor, you are an idiot. And Jon, you are a bigger idiot if you are listening to him. He has definitely read too much about Norse mythology or whatever."

Marc is defensive. "Oh yeah? Well, how do you explain three separate incidents then?"

"Easy!" she snaps back. "First of all, Mom and Dad were talking about that car for days before Grandpa moved in, and it was obviously going to Jon. Second, your English teacher loves Jon, and if there was anything true about what you said, he would give you the benefit of the doubt. Last but not least, have you seen or ever listened to a weather forecast? We have known about this storm for almost a week!"

Hmm ... all fair points.

Marc ponders it for a second then caves. "I guess you could be right. That all makes sense."

"Ya think?" Jill retorts, rolling her eyes. Then she puts in her ear pods so she can listen to her music the rest of the way home.

As we reach Marc's house to drop him off, he is a little bit down or deep in thought—I cannot really tell for sure—but I decide to try to cheer him up a little.

"Hey, I'll catch up with you tomorrow, assuming all this snow doesn't keep up and cause a full snow day."

He smiles as he hops out of the car.

"Text me later," I tell him, "so we can go over our homework notes, okay?"

"Sure thing. Thanks for the ride!"

As soon as he gets out of the car, Jill jumps into the front seat and smiles at me. "You weren't taking him seriously, were you?"

"Of course not," I scoff. "But he was happy about it, and who am I to take away his happiness?"

She shockingly agrees, saying, "Well, he also needs to not be living in a fantasy world where he could get himself into a situation he isn't prepared to handle. If he really believes that, it could put both of you in danger."

"How so?" I ask.

"Well, he could ask you to make up a rhyme that will let him safely jump off the roof of the school and fly or something and then—*boom!*" She says it as serious as a heart attack, but I know she is just dripping with sarcasm.

I give her a condescending look. "Now who is being the drama queen? Tell you what, if Marc asks me to make him fly, I'll refuse, okay? As for other dangers—I mean, it is Grinwell, Iowa, not a lot of super treacherous things happen in our part of the world."

When we reach the house and hop out of the car, I see a shovel waiting there, as a symbol of what I need to do next.

I shovel the driveway and sidewalk, which is wishful thinking, because it is coming down as fast as I can scoop it up, so I slide back inside into a nice, peaceful evening where everything is completely normal. Snowy, but normal.

Basement Buildout

Dustin

AS SOON AS I GET HOME and finish trying to clear the snow in the driveway, which is apparently part of my punishment because it keeps filling back up, I decided to actually do some homework. I mean, Coach is a jerk, but he's not wrong. If I let my grades slip, then I will be off the wrestling team and may potentially lose my chance at a scholarship, which is my way out of this hell.

I have always wanted to go to the University of Iowa, having been a fan of their wrestling teams since I was in sixth grade. They have such a rich, deep history. But, in order to get there, I have to focus. So, yes, I should focus on this stupid homework.

After a couple of hours of knuckling down, I am pretty much caught up in all my classes, or as close as I am going to get without talking to some of my teachers. So, I decide to head down to see what Coach is up to.

He isn't anywhere to be found, but then I hear a fair amount of noise coming from the basement. I might as well go down and check it out.

Sure enough, Coach is down there, setting something up. I have never seen anything like it, except for maybe in some old horror films. Somehow, this basement is transforming into some sort of Medieval torture chamber.

Coach sees me and says, "It's probably time for you to learn a bit about how all this works." He starts to describe what I am seeing, some of which is obvious.

There is a table in the middle of the room that looks like it came from a doctor's office that might have existed in the early 1900s. It is all wood with some cast iron cuffs and what looks like a crown at the top of it with a cuff for each arm on the sides and more cuffs for the feet at the bottom.

Next to the table is what looks a bit like an intravenous system you would see in a hospital, but much like the rest of this stuff, it looks quite old, as well. There is a big tube that starts at the floor and goes to the ceiling, and a large handheld pumping system that looks like the ball float valve in the back of a toilet, but much larger.

It looks like there are needles in the crown that appear to be used to extract or inject something into some poor sob. This thing looks wickedly interesting.

Coach starts to explain, "Back in the early 1900s, your great-great-grandfather created this system. It looks painful, but believe me; before this, it was much worse. As you may have guessed, we put the Asgardian on the table, and then we have to wait for him or her to reach the point of dehydration and exhaustion. Then we slow their heart rate way down with some propranolol. This is important, because until they reach this state, at least for most Asgardians, we won't be able to puncture their skin. We have to get them to the point where their durability and their quick healing capabilities are compromised if, in fact, those abilities have manifested for them.

"You see, an Asgardian has chemical messengers that deliver their essence to the rest of the body, similar to hormones that are released by the brain and distributed to the body through your blood. We both draw the blood and tap straight into the source of their essence in their brain in order to extract. Then we separate that essence into the blue serum you have seen after running what we extract through a special centrifuge, which causes everything to separate in a way similar to the white blood cells being separated from red blood cells, to extract plasma. This process is not quick and, once again, is dependent on a lot of factors, including the amount of essence we are able to extract, along with the overall health and capabilities of the Asgardian."

"How does anyone actually survive this process?" I ask.

"The trick is to leave just enough of their Asgardian essence in them for the extraction wounds to heal, but not enough that they remember what happened to them. This is a delicate balance. It varies a lot with age, as well as with the power of the line they descend from. The closer you get to Odin, the stronger they will be and the more essence they will have. If you guess wrong and they are human, though, there could be dire consequences, most likely resulting in paralysis or death." He hesitates then says, "It's also possible for you and I to heal the puncture wounds with a bit of our own magic, if we do make a mistake, so at least nobody can tell something unnatural happened to them. That is obviously critical."

I ask him further, "What does age have to do with it again?"

"Like most things, your Asgardian essence drains over time. Your peak levels start around sixteen, and when they fully degrade, you become human and die shortly thereafter, as you become susceptible to human diseases."

Ah, so now it makes sense why Coach is so focused on high school students and, to a certain extent, it explains why he is a high school wrestling coach and PE teacher when he has so many other options available to him with the power inside of him. He wants to find young Asgardians so he can maximize the yield compared to the risks of the process. Smart. This is also indirectly why it made sense for him to take out Coach Keith.

He then volunteers, "By taking the blue essence from others, we can slow this process down inside of us so we retain our powers for much longer. Ideally, we don't completely drain someone because we don't want their line to totally die; we want it to be weaker than ours. If their line completely dies, then we won't have a supply of our own to work with, and we won't live as long."

Well, that answers that question.

"So, we don't want to be the only line left?" I ask. "We want to be the strongest and have the most advantages?"

"Exactly. Maybe there is hope for you yet."

It's also interesting to note that this means I have more Asgardian essence in me than Coach does, and I could probably take him, unless he has been juicing up extra to be able to maintain a high level. I would definitely not put it past him to have a secret stash that only he has access to just in case he needs it.

I better be careful about that line of thought. He is a more formidable opponent than I want to take on, at least at this point.

"When did you use this equipment last?" I ask.

"I used it on an older Asgardian, so I didn't get much. I came as close as I have ever come to killing one of us."

I could almost sense that something went wrong last time, and it has Coach on edge. I will drop this for now, as it doesn't really matter anyway.

As I'm pondering that, Coach offers, "My first experience with this apparatus was when your great-grandfather showed me how it works. We had been chasing a descendant of Thor for weeks, and we were finally able to expose him, trap him, and start the extraction process. Unfortunately, we were wrong, and he was not an Asgardian. I had never seen a man die before my eyes. That's the type of thing you never forget. It's also why I am so insistent on being sure and proving that we have an Asgardian before we move to the extraction stage. If you don't stop it before that point, and you are wrong, then, within minutes, they *could* die. That is something you never forget."

No Alarm

Jon

AS THE NIGHT WORE ON, there was no more talk of superpowers or really anything at all out of the ordinary, except for the ridiculous amount of snow. This was one of those heavy, wet snows where every scoop of the shovel is met with resistance and is seriously difficult to budge. I much prefer the light, powdery snow. Unfortunately, we can't pick the type of snow we are going to get, so we deal with it as best we can.

Marc and I did text back and forth to make sure we got all our homework right, and yes, neither of us—namely me—didn't forget to do their homework. By the end of the night, I was caught up in every class and then some, and that is always my preferred mode of operation.

I am having trouble sleeping tonight. I keep dreaming that I have some mystical superpower and everyone is out to get me. I wake up several times, making an ear-piercing scream, only to find that Grandpa is still happily snoring away on his side of the room. I start to feel a little guilty about waking up so many times. Then again, he mumbles that rhyme in his sleep and snores so loudly.

As far as roommates go, I still think I have Grandpa beat right now. I'm glad he is here, though. It's nice to know that he is safe and taken care of by the people who love him the most.

I hear a noise and jump up. I'm pretty sure it's the front door opening, which means someone is leaving and I should be up already. I look at the time on my phone. Great, I am running super late. I need to leave to get Marc in about five minutes.

I throw on the closest clothes I can find then run to brush my teeth. I barely notice Mom standing in the kitchen as I run around her, trying to grab whatever I can for breakfast. I nab a banana, a Pop-Tart, and a bottle of water.

How can she be so calm? This is crazy. I could use a little help here; can't she see that? This is so weird. Okay, well, I guess that is all the time I have. I need to start the car and make sure there isn't any snow or ice on it.

I put on my coat and gloves then throw my book bag over my shoulder as I make my way to the door.

"Where are you going?" Mom asks.

"I have to warm up the car to get it ready for school." I mean, this should be obvious based on the time and the fact that I am clearly running so incredibly late.

"No, I didn't wake you because school was cancelled today due to the snow. Plus, you'll have a heck of a time getting out of that driveway. I just checked, and the snow plows haven't been by, so there is no chance any of us are going anywhere any time soon."

Oh. My. Goodness! Okay, now this all makes much more sense. With my alarm, I normally don't have any problems waking up in the morning, but on the rare occasion that I do forget to set it, or snooze it too many times, Mom always wakes me up to get ready for school in time.

"You can sit down and enjoy your Pop-Tart or something better, if you want. I figured we could organize the garage some today and possibly look for that genealogy book to help you with your next badge."

I'm still recovering from that running late panic attack, but I think that is a great idea! I am really looking forward to going through Grandpa and Grandma's things to get a glimpse at the book that Mom saw, as well as to see what other books they might have. I bet they have some original prints of some of the classics. Yes, this is a great plan and a great way to enjoy a snow day. I don't think I have been this excited to miss school ever.

"We will wait for your sister to get up so she can help us, as well," Mom declares.

I'm not so sure that Jill is going to be super excited to do that. In fact, I am almost positive she would sleep all day if Mom let her.

I see Mom texting her right now, which must be what wakes her most days and is super smart on Mom's part. It's much better to get a "*K*" response via text than it is to hear a grumpy voice first thing in the morning. At least that is true for me.

About fifteen minutes later, Jill comes trudging down the stairs and makes her way to the kitchen table. Mom silently walks over and sets her plate in front of her then backs away. Time to feed the animal. *Ha!*

"Thank you," Jill says. "And thank you for letting me sleep in this morning."

I guess one of the texts that Mom sent must have warned her about school being cancelled so Mom didn't have a repeat of my freak-out with Jill. Mom is always on top of everything.

After breakfast, Mom, Jill, and I head into the garage while Dad takes the task of clearing the snow this time. He is using a snow blower, which is a little bit like cheating, but I am certainly not going to complain. I bet it is going to be quite the challenge getting that heavy snow to go through the blower, though.

In the garage, to my surprise, Jill is almost more interested in helping than I am. She is organizing a lot of Grandma's things with Mom and finding out where different items have come from and which of our ancestors originally owned them. It's really interesting since Grandma had a lot of hobbies and collections of her own. She collected a lot of music, and Jill is seriously into music, dance, and all things entertaining like that. I guess maybe that is why she loves learning to play the piano and why she started with a dance company when she was six years old. She's actually really good at both, but I don't think

I tell her that enough. She has quite the gift and is really enjoying playing Grandpa and Grandma's old records on their antique record player while we look through everything. It is the perfect and seemingly appropriate mood music as we listen to jazz and look at so many items rich in history and our family culture.

We probably look through a dozen boxes before we reach some of Grandpa's old books. Now *this* is what I am talking about. There is an old poetry book in here, as well, that is leather bound and looks super ancient. I pull that out first and browse through the pages. Yep, there are a lot of poems in here, and one of them seems familiar. I recognize it as the one that Grandpa has been saying over and over. Well, at least we know where that comes from now. I am sure to point it out to Mom, although I doubt it is super important, just good to know.

The box also contains the book that Mom found. It's thick, and the family tree was hand-filled, going back centuries. What is interesting is that, when I go all the way to the back, I see that Jill is the last entry, and I am on the same page. It looks like this tree is current. That's great!

Mom helps me look through a couple hundred years of history, but her knowledge of the family drops off pretty quickly. I am going to have to read the rest from the notes that Grandpa has written throughout the book in the margins. This is going to be perfect for my genealogy badge, and I have no doubt this will be a huge factor in me earning that one.

The time goes by fast, and before I know it, we break for lunch to have sandwiches and to check on Grandpa, making sure he has everything he needs. Dad has been checking on him and taking care of him while we were in the garage, but we are going to need to help this afternoon so Dad can "take care of some work." Since he works in IT, he can do his work almost anywhere at any time. He just needs an internet connection.

In the afternoon, Jill decides to help Grandpa with a bit of grooming. She patiently helps Mom wash his hair then dries it and brushes it out. They even brush through his long beard. Jill is concerned with making Grandpa feel good about himself.

We get him dressed and looking pretty spiffy, and then we help him back into his chair and into the position he seems to love the most, which is staring out the window, watching people and cars pass our house. We don't know what he is looking for, but we know he is looking.

Snow Day

Dustin

WHEN MY ALARM GOES off, I hear the news on the classic rock station announce that school has been cancelled, so I take the opportunity to roll back over and try to fall back sleep for as long as I possibly can. I know Coach is up. I can hear him making a shake downstairs and a bunch of other noise. He clearly doesn't care at all that this is a snow day and, accordingly, I am entitled to some extra sleep and maybe even possibly a morning without an obnoxious shake to choke on. Then again, he isn't shouting up the stairs at me, so maybe that's what is happening after all.

I wake up a couple hours later and, for the first time in a long time, I feel totally rested. That was exactly what I needed—tons of sleep. I feel amazing, even without any additional blue essence. I'm good. Then I remember Coach's story about killing a human, and I'm right back in the middle of our quest to find an Asgardian.

I throw on some sweatpants and a sweatshirt, and then I head downstairs. There's a note on the refrigerator that says.

Morning sunshine,

Going ice fishing. As soon as you drink your shake and take your vitamins, clear the snow from the driveway and sidewalks. Do the driveway ALL THE WAY to the road. Then meet me on the lake. Track my cell.

ALL THE WAY to the road! Is he out of his ever-loving mind? That is something you call a plow to take care of for you, not something you have your kid do.

Okay, well, the only way to handle this is to go down and grab some blue essence and put that stuff to work. The sooner I get done with this task, the faster I can get back to planning and nosing around the house. I mean, the sooner I can go join Coach on the lake. Yeah right, I don't even like fishing in good weather.

Well, at least the snow has stopped, so I won't be doing this on repeat today.

I put on my coat, stocking hat, scarf, and the warmest gloves I have before getting started. I don't know if there is a Guinness world record for shoveling snow, but I think it might be possible that I set one. I am done with all the sidewalks and the whole driveway in under an hour, which buys me a little bit of snooping time.

I head down to the basement and start to look through everything I can find. There is an old chest in the corner with a padlock on it that is, of course, locked. I wonder where that key might be. I look around in boxes and on the shelves down, but it is nowhere to be found. Then I do what any sane person would do and run a web search, looking for videos on how to pick a lock on a chest. There are hundreds of videos. Perfect.

It takes me about a dozen different videos and a solid hour of fiddling with it until I am finally able to successfully hear it pop out and unlock.

I opened the top to find a bunch of books, papers, and a few artifacts, like an old, dirty Viking helmet, not the pro football team, but an actual real Viking helmet that is authentic as hell and badass.

I pull out a book, and on the cover, it says, "*Asgardian Protection Society*." Skimming through it, I find its rules and guidelines for the descendants of Asgardians. Interesting.

It turns out that there is some sort of agency that registers Asgardians and establishes rules to make sure that other Asgardians are safe and don't do things that fall outside of the established rules of the society. There are a lot of rules in here, too. For example:

1) A descendant of Asgard shall not reveal his lineage to a human authority or medical personnel.

2) A descendant of Asgard shall not harm any other descendant of Asgard, or risk the termination of his entire line of descendants.

There are so many rules that I start to lose track, but I know I have either already violated some of them or am planning on violating them. Therefore, I am going to ignore this thing. Also, it is super old, so whoever came up with these things, I'm sure they are long gone by now.

I can't really ask Coach about it because, well, then he would know I was snooping around in his stuff again, and we all know how that worked out last time. Hard pass.

Of course, I am definitely trying that Viking helmet on.

It looks exactly as sick on me as it did sitting in the chest. I take a couple of selfies quickly with the camera on my phone then put it back in the chest with everything else. I do my best to put everything back exactly the way I found it, but I'm not one hundred percent sure that I'm successful.

Then I realize I have to figure out how to relock the chest without a key. This sends me back to the web to search for how to do that. I spend far too long on that when it turns out that it locks simply by pushing in on the part of the lock that had popped out when I picked it. I'm such an idiot.

Now that half the day is gone, I run up to make a few sandwiches to take to the lake. Even though I really don't want to go, Coach's request to join him isn't optional.

I pack everything into a backpack, along with a thermos of fresh, hot coffee for Coach, then track Coach on my phone as I head to the lake to get this over with as quickly as possible.

Coach has a little shelter setup in the middle of the lake, so I head out there to see the hole he has made in the ice. He has already caught a fish and, unless I am mistaken, that is likely to be our dinner tonight.

"Is that our dinner?" I ask to find out.

"No, it's mine. You are going to need to catch your own, Locke."

Great. I would love to do that. Thanks, *Dad*.

He hands me a short pole that I reluctantly take then drop the line down into the hole. Then I wait and wait.

"How long did it take you to catch that one?" I ask Coach, but he doesn't respond, probably meaning he has no idea. I mean, he has been out here four or five hours at least, so this isn't going to be super-fast. It all makes me think: who is it that thought this whole idea up? Hey, you want to go fish in the freezing cold? Sure, but how do we get to the fish? The lake is frozen. How about we cut a hole in it and stick a worm down in the freezing cold water and see what happens? Imagine their shock, and then how proud they were of themselves when it actually worked!

After a while, I ask Coach, "Are there any rules to what Asgardians can and cannot do, or any people who do what we do that I need to be aware of?"

"Well, no, we have never really listened to anyone or been into the rules. It's not our style." He continues, "There used to be this group that *thought* they could tell everyone what to do and how to act, but nobody has heard from them in decades. If they are still around, they are irrelevant."

I am pretty convinced he believes that, so I guess that book came from that group and is as pointless as I thought.

"Why do you ask?" he questions.

"I wanted to know in case there was someone out there who was going to bust my balls, but I guess I probably have watched too many movies. Thanks for setting me straight." Sometimes, I think he can read my mind and that he somehow already knows that I looked in his chest. If he isn't going to bring it up, though, I sure am not going to. That is just going to need to be left up in the air.

It takes me a few more hours to finally catch a little crappie. Coach already left by that time to go back to the house to clean his fish and fry it up.

I don't want to eat this thing, but I am going to at least take it with me so I can show Coach I got the job done. He is the type who will send you right back out the door if you don't do what he says, and there is no chance I am taking that risk. So, the fish comes with me.

Coach is already done with his dinner by the time I get back, and he laughs at my little fish but allows it since, technically, he didn't say how big the fish needed to be.

There is nothing on this thing to eat, so I am going to open up a can of beans and maybe make myself another protein shake. I'm certainly not eating that fish. I guess I will go to bed a little hungry tonight. It doesn't matter.

We didn't get any more snow, so tomorrow, we should be back in school, and then I can finally wrestle Thor.

The Challenge

Jon

THE NEXT MORNING GOES much more smoothly. As expected, school is back on, so we do our normal morning routine then grab our bags and coats and head out to the car. This time, I don't warm it up for Jill, figuring, if I can be cold for a minute, she can be, too. Plus, she is wearing the thickest wool sweater I have ever seen, so there is no way she could possibly be cold.

We spend a little bit of time talking about yesterday, which was a really great day. After dinner, we played dominoes until bedtime, and I realized it had been a while since we had a family game night. It was fun, even if Jill and Mom totally destroyed Dad and me.

Once the car is warm enough to not fog over with every breath we take, we pull out of the driveway.

When we pick up Marc, I notice something strange about him. He isn't wearing anything with Thor on it. Instead, he is wrapped up in a normal-looking brown suede winter jacket and just has jeans and a school sweatshirt on, so literally everything is similar to what I wear and nothing even moderately resembles his favorite Norse hero. Not to mention, he is using a plain, old, black backpack. It's a good look, but disturbing at the same time.

"Is everything okay?" I ask.

He shrugs. "Yeah, everything is fine." Then he turns and looks out the window for the rest of the ride, which is oddly quiet.

Something pretty big is on his mind, but I don't know what it is right now. It's probably better, anyway, because there is still quite a bit of snow on the road, and I need to focus on the drive more than normal, especially in intersections where the snow paths meet and the tracks are less easy to line up with your tires.

After we drop off Jill, he decides to come clean and says, "I figured I need to keep a low profile if I am going to be your sidekick, right? I don't want to draw any attention to your powers."

I shake my head, realizing Marc is, in fact, okay and as delusional as ever.

Getting my mind off his delusions, I think about school. I'm sure everyone is a little disappointed that the snow days didn't continue and we have a full day today, but it was really great for me, as I am totally ready for every class.

Walking into English is like a broken record from the last class. Everything is going fine, and then Dustin walks in and, for the second time, he kicks me to a seat in the back of the room. I don't really care, to be honest. From my perspective, the more space between the two of us, the better.

Every once in a while, he whispers something to Marc, and it's clearly not good, going by how Marc twists in his seat to look back at me with those scared puppy dog eyes of his. Unfortunately, I can't be much help against Dustin, as we have already witnessed. Then it hits me.

I bet he is talking about gym class today and what he is going to do to Marc. Yeah, that would definitely cause that type of reaction from him.

Marc does not have any desire to be in a fight or do anything remotely physical, so wrestling with Dustin would be pretty low on his to-do list.

After class, Marc stays in his seat, so I do the same until everyone is gone. Then I walk up to him and ask, "What was Dustin whispering to you?"

"He was basically reminding me of everything he plans to do to me in gym class. He kept saying, *Thor, I'm going to drop the hammer on you.*" Marc is shaking a bit. "I don't think I can do it, Jon. I think I might say I'm sick and try to go home."

I shrug. "You know, though, you can't do that forever. Maybe it is better for you to hold your ground or at least go through with it to get it over with."

"I know you are right," he admits, "but it doesn't make it any easier."

I CONNECT WITH MARC again at lunch and see that he is either purposefully eating light to not have too much food in his stomach or he lost his appetite at some point today. I don't know which it is, but I do know that he is more afraid than I have seen him in a long time, and we have been in some scary situations. We have been chased by big dogs, a swarm of bees, and suffered through rock climbing in the Scouts together. None of that had him looking this way. And he is now begging with me.

"Can you try a rhyme on me, just to see if will work? You are really my last and only hope, Jon."

I hesitantly agree, but I also say, "If I do this, you cannot hold it against me if it doesn't work."

Marc smiles in relief. "Agreed."

I go with something quick, right off the top of my head.

"As we sit around this table,
Give Marc the wisdom,
To be able to defeat Dustin,
And know his every move.
To counter them with strength,
As he keeps his footwork in the groove."

Marc is satisfied with this. He pats me on the shoulder, and then we are off to get ready for wrestling.

The Plan

Dustin

SITTING ALONE IN THE cafeteria, I aggressively chew through the cardboard pizza , thinking the topping is supposed to be some sort of sausage, but it really could be any kind of meat. It had almost no flavor whatsoever.

It's actually impressive seeing as how you can usually at least taste the tomato sauce on pizza. It could also be due to the crazy fast speed I am eating it with, wanting a bit of time prior to the wrestling practice to talk with Coach and come up with a plan for testing Marc. I want to ask him a few more questions about how, in the past, he may have been able to tell if he was wrestling an Asgardian.

Then I am held up a bit in lunch, talking with Jess about Brad.

"Brad is doing much better now. It was nice that we had a snow day to give him a little bit of time to get settled in at home, even if it was a slippery ride from the hospital. He won't be in school for a while, but I'll take his homework to him every night and help him as best I can."

While she talks, I do my best to act like I am paying attention. I have to admit she is a pretty good friend, clearly, to be doing all of this for Brad. That must be nice for Brad—to know he has someone like that.

"Dustin," she continues, "I don't want you to take this the wrong way, but I really think you should stop trying so hard to impress everyone. Stunts like you pulled in the weight room can only lead to problems."

Well, she is right about that. I do have problems. Basically, I found out that neither her or Brad are useful to me, and that is a big problem. I decide to interrupt her.

"You know what? Coach said he needs to talk to me before my next class. Thanks for the advice, though. I appreciate it. I'll try to be more careful." I think that might have almost sounded sincere, so I guess the coast is clear and I can make my getaway.

I drop my tray off and throw my silverware in the giant metal bowl of soapy water. Then I head straight to the locker room.

I am nervous, which is an interesting feeling. It might be that I am nervous because we are running low on victims—I mean, prospects—right now. I am as nervous for this class as I was at the state wrestling tournament last year. I had a pretty big opponent there, as well. In fact, I had lost to him earlier in the year before I turned sixteen, so the tournament was my chance to prove myself. Just like today, I feel the need to prove myself to Coach. I doubt I will ever get over that feeling, but I guess that might be what Jess was talking about. I keep trying to get his attention and praise.

Well, the championship match last year was neck and neck. I would get a takedown, he would escape. He would take me down, I would escape. It kept going on like that for the entire match. As regulation ended, he escaped with what I thought was no time left on the clock, but he got away, anyway, sending the match into the first tie-breaker.

We kept battling back and forth, and this went on all the way to a *third* tie-breaker. For whatever reason, I took him down and held him down. And with that hold, I moved on to victory. It was exhausting, but one of the best feelings I have ever felt. I truly earned that win and, at least in my eyes, I earned some respect from Coach.

Today is another chance to prove myself to Coach, if we can figure out how to trigger the Thor in Marc.

I finish lacing up my wrestling shoes. I know it is just gym class, but since we are wrestling, I wear these instead of my regular gym shoes.

It's the natural thing for me to do. Not wearing them would be like a football player wearing slippers to a football game or something. It wouldn't feel right, even if they did exceptionally well.

When I get to the wrestling room, Coach is the only person there, which is perfect.

"How can I tell if Marc is from Thor when we wrestle?" I ask him what's been on my mind.

"Hi, Locke, it's nice to see you, too. I'm fine. Thanks for asking." He does this when he thinks I don't greet him with "respect."

I keep looking at him with expectant eyes, urging him to answer the question. He made his point.

"So, when I have wrestled with other Asgardians, it was something I felt. It's like they can anticipate your moves, and they can match you step for step. By now, you know that is unusual, unless you are holding back. But the biggest indicator is if you literally cannot win. A descendant of Thor can be incredibly strong.

"If Miller is faster and stronger than you, and there is literally nothing you can do about it, then we will know. Don't make this any harder than it needs to be. Let's face it, though; that kid is most likely *not* going to be able to do anything. We are just testing him because he is available to test. It is out of pure convenience and a bit of desperation."

He's right; Miller has never acted with any sort of courage or confidence that would come from being freakishly strong. In fact, every interaction I have had with him has been the exact opposite. He only exhibits weakness in every possible way, both physically and mentally.

Now I am less excited. Coach has burst my bubble, but reasonably so. I mean, this is Marc Miller we are talking about. What was I thinking? *Ha*!

Eureka

Jon

AS WE WALK TO THE WRESTLING room, I check in with Marc. "Are you ready for this? You know, you can say you aren't feeling well, if you want."

He shakes his head. "No, I am as ready as I'll ever be, and I feel really great right now. Probably because of you. Thanks again!"

I am suddenly not so sure about this, afraid that Marc has a false sense of confidence and that he is about to get his world rocked. At the same time, I don't want to burst his bubble. I mean, he does seem to be feeling great right now. He might as well have a couple of moments to feel that way before the inevitable.

Unfortunately, Dustin is already in the wrestling room when we get there, so my secret hope that he somehow got food poisoning or something didn't happen.

He is talking with Coach Locke, no doubt going over the drills for the day and exactly what he wants Dustin to show everyone.

As soon as we get there, Dustin lets out, "There he is. All right, Thor, are you ready for me to show everyone how this is done?"

Marc turns and looks at me with a bit of fear in his eyes, but when he sees me, he firms up and turns back to Dustin, saying, "Let's do this!"

This, of course, causes Dustin to laugh and mock him. "*Let's do this! Ha!*"

Everyone in class takes a seat, and Coach Locke steps into the center of the mat.

149

"Today, we are going to learn a counter move to a basic snap down. These are both common and important to be aware of. I would actually say the snap down is in the top three moves that good wrestlers have in their arsenal. You have to be really fast to stop it." He looks around the room, clearly making sure everyone is paired up.

I was fortunate enough to get paired up with the only other person in the class about our size, and her name is Sara Klein. She is a bit lanky for a girl but freakishly strong and has been known to be a bit of a tomboy, which she is apparently completely fine with. I have no doubt she is going to be delivering some punishment to me, but at least she isn't Dustin.

"Okay, Locke," Coach Locke says, "you and your partner, Mr. Miller here, will come up now and demonstrate the basic snap down. I'll explain the defense later."

Dustin can't get to the center fast enough, whereas Marc takes his sweet time, confidently strolling behind Dustin.

They get into the center, and then Coach begins, "You start with your arms around each other's necks, and then one person reaches up and pulls the other one down onto the mat while popping their hips back to make room for their opponent's face to hit the mat and then he takes their back. I'll show you the defense in a minute. Show them, Locke."

Dustin grabs Marc and attempts to jerk him down, but Marc drops to both knees, closes the distance, and does a double leg takedown, pinning Dustin.

Everyone in the room is completely dumbfounded. We all look at each other for a second then start clapping and cheering, "Way to go, Miller!"

That was a wild and totally awesome sight to see!

"Have you done this before, Miller?" Coach Locke asks. "That was excellent and is essentially the perfect defense to a snap down. Great work, son! Let's switch it up. Miller, you do the snap down."

Dustin and Marc lock up like they did before then circle each other for what seems like forever, but it is really only a couple of times before Marc pulls Dustin down with his face slamming into the mat hard then Marc takes his back.

When he looks up at Coach Locke, I'm not sure which of them has a more shocked expression on their faces. Dustin, on the other hand, is super pissed and clearly ready to go again.

They do this for a few more rounds, and each time, Marc destroys Dustin. It is literally the craziest thing I have ever seen. Then, all of a sudden, Marc has become some sort of wrestling genius, even though, to my knowledge, he has never had any training.

Everyone congratulates Marc by patting him on the back and telling him how amazing he looked.

Marc glances over to me and mouths, "*Thank you.*"

I point back at him and tell him, "That's all you, buddy. Nice job!"

We are all feeling pretty good about what we all saw. Well, except for Dustin, who is over talking with Coach, who is checking out his nose, which is bleeding from the last time his face was planted into the mat. Then we hear Coach Locke yell at Dustin, "Locke, in my office *now*!"

They walk off, and then we hear him yell at Dustin, "What exactly do you think you are doing? You let a kid like that, with no experience, totally destroy you *repeatedly*! What is wrong with you? Are you just going to be a total loser now!"

Dustin sounds defeated as he says, "He was freakishly fast and strong, Coach." Then he says something strange. "I think we found one."

I guess Coach is still recruiting for the wrestling team.

Sure enough, Coach Locke opens the door and says, "Class dismissed. Miller, come to my office."

Marc and I look at each other, and then we both shrug.

"I'll see you at the Corolla after school," I tell him then tease, "Have a nice chat with Coach Locke, superstar."

He smiles the widest smile I have ever seen and quietly says, "You know that was all because of you, right? There is no way I could have done that without your rhyme."

I shake my head, grinning. "I think maybe it was just great timing, and it gave you the confidence to do what you already knew you could do." With that, I head to the lockers to get ready for my next class, and Marc marches into Coach Locke's office.

Asgardian's Collection

Dustin

I AM STILL A BIT SHOCKED that Marc took me down. I really was planning to eliminate him as a prospect. This is significantly better, though. Now we can move forward with our plan, and I can see exactly how this whole process works.

I start by asking him, "So, you have never wrestled before, right?"

He shrugs. "Only in gym class. Never for real."

"If you don't mind me asking, then how did you know those moves and how did you get strong enough to throw me around like that?"

"Honestly," he says, "I really don't know. It was like something took over, almost like it was magic or something."

"C'mon, Miller"—I grin—"that doesn't happen. You can just shoot straight with us."

He shrugs.

I can see that we are getting nowhere fast.

I look over at Coach, who decides to take a crack at getting Marc to talk.

"Miller, did anyone in your family ever wrestle, or do you know much about your background and where your family originated from?"

He seems to ponder this. "I'm not totally sure if anyone wrestled, but we sure don't talk about it. I think maybe my family came here from somewhere in Europe, but that was several generations ago."

"My understanding is the kids call you *Thor*," Coach says. "Can you tell me more about that?"

"Well, I like Norse stories, and especially those about Thor and Loki. Every year for Halloween, I still dress up as Thor. Honestly, most kids call me that to make fun of me, but I don't care at all."

"I see," Coach says. "Well, I'm actually a big collector of things from Asgard. Would you like to see my collection?"

"Sure!" Marc brightens up, not looking so nervous anymore. "That would be cool! I mean, yes, Coach Locke."

Coach then says, "Okay, well, I don't have any more periods left to teach, so let's go now. I'll write you a note to get you out of your classes for the rest of the day."

Marc shrugs, looking nervous again. "Okay, I guess."

A few minutes later, we all pile into Coach's truck and pull out of the school parking lot, making our way through town.

I'm beginning to understand why Coach rented this little crappy house in the middle of nowhere now. I'm not exactly sure how this is going to go down, but not having to worry about people hearing any strange noises is going to be an advantage, for sure.

Before we get there, I decide to talk with Marc some more.

"I'm sorry that I was rough on you. I didn't know that you had that kind of ability in you. If I had known that, I would have worked with you instead of against you."

"It's okay," Marc says. "I actually get that kind of treatment pretty often from everyone except Jon. Speaking of Jon, are we going to be back before school lets out? I need to text him to let him know I won't be riding with him if we aren't back in time."

I quickly say, "Oh, I'm sure we can have you back, right, Coach?"

Coach nods. "Yeah, definitely won't be a problem. It's a small town. After we show you our collection, we can buzz you right back over to the school."

This seems to satisfy Marc, as he puts his cell phone down.

As soon as we get to our place, I offer to make Marc a protein shake. "I figure you're probably tired after kicking my butt today and could use a fill up."

"Actually," he says, "I am getting kind of hungry, so that sounds good."

I grab all the usual ingredients—bananas, peanut butter, protein powder, and one of our special ingredients—and blend it all up.

When Marc takes it, I say, "Bottoms up. You have to drink that one fast for the protein to kick in."

He shrugs, looking at it curiously. "Okay, sure. I wasn't planning to sip it, anyway. It doesn't taste amazing, but I haven't had many protein shakes."

I look at him and cheer him on until he downs the whole thing. Then I wash everything out and make a shake for myself, as well, so it doesn't seem too weird.

About that time, Coach calls from downstairs, "Boys, come on down here so I can show you what we have."

We head down the stairs, and Marc starts taking a look around.

Coach has taken out some shields and old scrolls with writing on them, and pretty much whatever junk he could scrounge up, it seems. He even pulls out that cool Viking helmet.

Then Marc's eyes fall on the table, and he says, "Whoa! What is that?"

Coach explains, "Well, it's a table that they say was used to extract the essence of Asgardian's from their body. Do you want to see how it was done?"

"Sure," Marc says. "But we don't have anyone from Asgard."

Coach laughs. "Why don't you hop up there?"

Marc jumps up and lies down.

Perfect. I have to admit that Coach is clever.

Coach starts to circle the table as he says, "So, they would circle the table then place these cuffs on the arms, and these on the legs." As

Coach says each step of the process that he is performing, he effectively locks Marc up without a fight. "They are a special metal that is imbued with magic to keep the Asgardian still." He steps over to the machine then says, "They also have been fed propranolol to slow their heart rate down a bit."

"Coach Locke, this is kind of freaking me out. Can you let me out?" Marc asks.

"Sure," Coach says. "Just tell me who you descend from, and I can get this all over with in a jiffy."

Marc's eyes widen. He looks absolutely terrified. "Um, Sue and Tom Miller?"

Coach barks out loudly, almost like his voice echoes. "Which son of Odin do you descend from?"

Marc starts crying. "Coach Locke, I don't know what you are talking about."

"What is your secret?" Coach asks. "If you tell us yours, we will tell you ours. Either way, we aren't leaving here until we know your origin and extract your essence, Asgardian!"

Missing Man

Jon

SO, WORD SPREAD PRETTY fast through the school of how Marc Miller, also known as Thor, was able to easily take down and pin the state wrestling champ. It is pretty funny to hear everyone talking about him in a respectful way versus how they usually make fun of him. He must be loving this right now!

I have to admit that I certainly saw that going down in a completely different way. After all, Dustin manhandled me, so I know how strong he is firsthand, and that makes me respect what Marc did even more. It's no small thing to make it look so easy to take out someone clearly as good as Dustin. It's so hard to believe, in fact, that I start to wonder if what I said didn't actually have something to do with it. I know that Marc completely believes it did, but I have to agree with Jill—that sounds crazy. Even thinking this seems ridiculous. I need to shake that thought.

As the final bell rings, I start looking forward to hearing how Marc's afternoon went after his victory in gym class.

I head out to the Corolla to get it warmed up. Then I sit and listen to whatever happens to be on the radio. It's taking Marc forever to get to the car. Everyone is probably wanting to talk to him and congratulate him on his big victory. I text him to let him know I am waiting for him and have the car nice and warm. No response.

So, I continue to sit there and wait patiently until the Corolla is the only car left in the parking lot. This is really strange and not like Marc. He is never late. He knows that I also have to pick up Jill.

Oh Jill, I need to text her to let her know I am running behind schedule really quick. I then text Marc one last time.

Where are you? I text.

Again, no answer.

I better go back into the school and try to hunt him down.

I walk through the empty hallways, only hearing an occasional locker slam shut but never anywhere near where Marc would be. Since he isn't in any of his classes and the last place I saw him was in the wrestling room, I head that way to see if he went back there to talk to Coach Locke some more now that there would be no time constraint with classes. When I get there, however, all the lights are off and no one is around.

I catch up with one of the wrestlers and ask him, "Where is Coach Locke and the rest of the wrestlers?"

The guy shrugs. "Coach Locke gave us the night off to prepare for challenges tomorrow."

Oh right, challenges. I read about this once in the school paper. Challenges are when the various wrestlers in the same weight class compete with each other for the right to represent the school in the next meet. I guess that rules out the wrestling room and Coach Locke.

I really can't wait any longer, so I text Marc again, telling him to contact me if he needs a ride because I have to pick up Jill.

As I head over to the middle school, I can't help but feel that something is really off. This has never happened in the entire time I have known Marc. He rides with us every day to and from school. There are no exceptions. Not ever.

When I get to the middle school, Jill is looking at me with one hand on her hip and her customary stout scowl on her face.

She opens the passenger door and complains, "It's about time! What took you so long?"

"I can't find Marc," I quickly snap back. "I have no idea where he is, and I'm starting to get worried about him."

"Yeah, well, I'm sure Mom and Dad are getting worried about us since you are already almost half an hour late picking me up."

I actually didn't think about that. I could get in some trouble for being late.

Great, another thing to worry about!

Sure enough, when we get home, Mom and Dad are both waiting for us.

"I was about to drive over to the schools to look for you two. What took so long? Did you have problems with the Corolla?" Dad asks.

"No, Jon was over half an hour late picking me up because he lost his little buddy," Jill complains.

"Marc didn't meet you at the car?" Mom asks. She knows how odd that is.

I shake my head, worry tingeing my voice when I tell her, "No, and I am really worried about him. This isn't like him, Mom. You know as well as I do that Marc wouldn't miss meeting me."

Mom agrees. "Yes, that is strange. I'll call his mom and see if she has heard from him. Maybe he got picked up from school early."

Relieved to have someone helping me, I thank her for that. Then I head into the house to drop off my bag and grab a quick snack. I plan to get back out there to look for Marc.

As I munch on an apple and drink a quick soda, Mom comes in and says, "I talked to Marc's mom, and he said the wrestling coach wanted to take Marc out for a snack and a talk. Apparently, Marc texted her to ask if it was okay and she said yes." She cocks her head in confusion. "Do you have any idea why?"

Well, that is awfully strange, but I guess it kind of makes sense. Still, Marc could have texted me, as well, to give me a heads-up so I wouldn't worry and wait forever. Maybe he didn't know how long it would take?

I tell Mom, "Marc actually beat Dustin, Coach Locke's son and the state wrestling champion, in gym class today. He was a perfect wrestling machine. I have never seen him do anything remotely close to that before."

Mom smiles widely. "Maybe he finally found his thing. Stranger things have happened. Sometimes kids are late bloomers. I could definitely see that with Marc."

Hearing that, Jill mocks, "Maybe it was your *superpowers*."

"What did you say?" Mom asks.

I quickly interject, "Nothing, Mom. Jill is giving me a hard time for something Marc made up the other day."

She carries on with getting dinner ready and ignores our sibling feud.

I give Jill the evil eye. Everyone knows what is said in the car stays in the car. She needs to keep her big mouth shut.

I decide to head into the living room to play a few video games before dinner and unwind a bit after a long day.

I see Grandpa is there, in his usual position, which means he is staring aimlessly out the window, mumbling his rhyme and seeming to be in his own world.

I dive head-first into a battle on my game and am lost in a cyber world where I hunt down guns and supplies that I can use to last as long as possible. Still, I have a nagging feeling about Marc in the back of my mind. I'm sure he's fine if he is with Coach Locke. I just hope Dustin doesn't get the bright idea to avenge his loss from earlier today.

The Helper

Dustin

MARC BEGS, "WHAT ESSENCE? Are you going to kill me, Coach Locke? Please don't kill me. I didn't mean to beat Dustin. I'm sorry."

Coach laughs. "Ha, this is not about some wresting loss. We came to this town, following a lead that I picked up that someone here could be ascending."

Marc looks confused. "Coach Locke, I have no idea what you are talking about. You are scaring me. This isn't funny."

"I am dead serious, Miller. I need to get some answers. You see, Dustin and I descend from Loki's line, which is what gives us so much strength, speed, and durability. You must descend from a son of Odin to be able to defeat one of us."

"I don't understand what you are saying." Marc shakes his head. "I just dress up like Thor for Halloween. Are you saying this is real?"

"Locke," Coach says, "bend this steel rod to prove it to Miller here."

"No problem, Coach." I grab the rod from him and, sure enough, it is super easy to bend.

"Can you start from the beginning?" Marc asks, eyes wide on the steel rod that I should not have been able to bend so easily, if I was normal. "How did this happen to both of you, and what brought you here again?"

Coach sighs. It seems like this is going to take some time, but he is willing to humor Miller for some reason. Personally, I don't think this is a good idea, but I kind of want to hear what he has to say, as well.

Coach starts, "For centuries, ever since Asgardians came to earth, there have been descendants, sometimes called demi-gods, who were offspring of an Asgardian and a human. Some generations are skipped, but when a potential heir reaches sixteen, they either ascend or they do not. If they ascend, they inherit some or all of the powers that come from their heritage.

"This is exactly what happened to me, and then to my son, Locke. He is actually a year older than all of you, as he started school a year late because his mom wanted to give him a size advantage. So, he turned sixteen last year, ascended, and won the state championship.

"Now, all of us have some amount of essence available once we ascend, and if we continue to use it, it will deplete over time. Our line was forced to determine a few centuries ago that we could extract and consume the essence of other Asgardians to retain and refill our essence. So, we have been hunting down and extracting this in the form of a blue serum, which we freeze then consume on a regular basis. We call this serum *blue essence*." He stops to see if this is registering with Marc, who seems to be a captive audience, no pun intended.

Coach admits, "We came here because I extracted what I could from an old man a few weeks ago, and he had a yearbook and some pictures from Grinwell High School that were current. His wife interrupted us before I could grab him, and so I had to put her down before taking him and extracting almost everything from him so he would forget what happened. He was from Bragi's line, the second son of Odin. He was using an alias, which was pretty smart, because we didn't exactly know who to come after here, but then we happened upon you, I presume a descendant of Thor."

"Why are you telling me all this?"

Coach sighs. "We really are just confirming the line you are from because, if you are from Thor's line, then there is another Asgardian around here from Bragi's, and we want both of you. Plus, after we are done with you, you aren't going to remember this, anyway."

Coach continues, "In order to make it reasonable for me to start looking around here, in Grinwell, I needed to be a part of the school. I approached Coach Keith to see if he was thinking of retiring or making a change and, well, he said no. Of course, that didn't work for me, so I had to take matters into my own hands, literally, and retire him another way."

Marc elevates his state of panic and says, "Coach Locke, I am not an Asgardian, and I don't have any special powers or abilities, so what is this going to do to me?"

"Well, we know that you couldn't have beaten Dustin if you didn't have some Asgardian essence in you, so you should be fine. If you were totally human, though, then this will be painful at a minimum and most likely lethal."

I cut in, "You see, it's really important that you tell us what you know. Your life could literally depend upon it."

Marc considers this for a moment then starts describing every comic book, novel, and movie he has read or seen related to Asgard, which turns out to be a lot. In fact, there are so many of them that I just walk away for a bit to clear my head and think of what the next step should be.

I'm not sure if Marc is what we are after, but I am positive that he should not have been able to beat me if Big John couldn't do it. There is no way that makes sense unless he had some kind of help.

I'm beginning to wonder if it's possible for us to somehow empower a human with our abilities or if they will only work on us. I think this question is important enough to interrupt Coach.

I walk back into the room as Marc drones on and ask, "Coach, can I see you for a minute?"

Coach walks with me upstairs where I ask him, "Do you know if it's possible for us to empower a human for a short period of time? Is it possible that the person who is an Asgardian somehow made Marc strong enough to defeat me?"

He thinks about it for a minute. "Honestly, I have never tried, and I don't think it would be possible for us or for Thor's line to do that, but possibly Bragi's line. Bragi's poetry has always had an effect on humans when spoken by one of them."

This is a massive concern at this point, and I have to voice it. "I think it's possible that Marc had some help to defeat me. Maybe we should find that out before going any further with the process. We could be wasting our time."

Coach thinks about it then says, "There was definitely one time at a school when I experienced that effect firsthand. A descendant of Bragi was a male cheerleader, and every time they did a specific cheer, their team would score either a touchdown or a field goal. Most people chalked it up to the positive attitude of the crowd rubbing off on the team. To this day, though, they still try to use that same cheer when their team is down yet, without that Bragi to say it with them, it has no effect unless by chance they get lucky and the team was already going to score. It's kind of sad if you think about it and a bit of a mean trick that the Bragi played on them. They thought their positive attitude was making the difference when, in fact, it was the reciting of a poem by a Bragi that brought their success. Seeing as we are chasing a Bragi now, it is possible that we could have experienced something similar earlier in the day."

Enough is Enough

Jon

I PLAY THE GAME UNTIL dinner then help wheel Grandpa into the dining room to eat. Mom made meatloaf, mashed potatoes, corn, and peaches, which is normally a meal that I cannot get enough of. Today, though, everything tastes off. I can't shake the feeling that something is up with Marc.

I don't understand why he hasn't called or texted me yet. I mean, if he is spending time with Dustin, I'm sure he has a story or two to tell me about his whole afternoon.

What a weird turn of events. Suddenly, because of one gym class, Dustin and Coach Locke are super interested in Marc. It's bizarre.

As dinner finishes up, I take my dishes to the kitchen to rinse them off and slide them into the dishwasher, literally going through the motions. Then I head back to the dining room, having to say something.

"Mom, Dad, I can't shake the feeling that something is up with Marc. He never goes this long without a call, text, or something. What did Mrs. Miller say that Coach Locke and Dustin wanted to do with him again?"

"They went to grab a snack or something," Mom answers. "I'm sure everything is fine. He is a teacher and a coach, and he has his son with them, too."

I question, "But what do we know about Coach Locke really, other than he has a great coaching record?"

Right about that time, Grandpa starts moaning super loudly, and Mom says, "Can you please move Grandpa back into the living room and let him look out the window?"

"Sure, it would be my pleasure," I tell her, heading over to Grandpa.

"Dad and I have to run to watch Jill's dance practice tonight, as they are getting ready for a big competition and need a crowd, so I need you to watch Grandpa."

"Sure, that's fine," I tell her, wheeling Grandpa out of the dining room. "I don't have any plans, anyway, especially with no word from Marc."

Of course, as soon as they pull out of the driveway, Grandpa starts repeating, "I once heard some words that unlocked my brain. It cleared up the fog so I could think again. I once heard some words that unlocked my brain. It cleared up the fog so I could think again. I ONCE HEARD SOME WORDS THAT UNLOCKED MY BRAIN. IT CLEARED UP THE FOG SO I COULD THINK AGAIN!"

Grandpa is getting super loud and repeating it over and over.

Finally, I snap.

"Enough is enough, Grandpa! I get it. *I once heard some words that unlocked my brain. It cleared up the fog so I could think again.*"

Grandpa then says something new ...

He gasps, and I swear he says, "You. You. YOU!"

I have to think for a second, and then I get it. "Ah! *You* once heard some words that unlocked *your* brain. It cleared up the fog so *you* could think again."

At that second, Grandpa takes an even bigger breath of air, and then he looks me straight in the eye and says, "I knew it was you. You saved me, Jon! Thank you!"

I literally about pass out, and not because of the compliment but because he actually said something other than that same rhyme. I'm so happy!

"Grandpa! It's so great to hear you say something other than that rhyme!"

"I was hoping someone with the power would hear it and repeat it and, sure enough, you did."

"What do you mean, Grandpa?" I ask. "Are you sure you're okay?"

He smiles brightly. "I am now." Then his smile fades as he looks down, seeming to be deep in thought. "You must have had your birthday ..." He meets my eyes again. "Which means you may have started to notice that, when you say some poems, things seem to come true, right?"

I'm hesitant, but I eventually say, "How ...? How did you know that? I mean, it was only a few times, but yeah, there have been some strange coincidences."

Grandpa nods. "It's not a coincidence, Jon. The only coincidence is the last name you inherited from your father, since my family changed theirs generations ago to protect us. Unless ... Unless you have inherited the line from both sides. Hmm... I will have to ponder that. Anyway, you have *the gift*. Every generation has the possibility of getting it but, for some reason, it skipped your mother. I'm so glad, though, that you have it, as my essence was really low, and then ... they took it."

"What do you mean by *essence*, Grandpa?" Maybe Grandpa isn't okay. Yeah, he is talking again, but what he is saying sounds crazy.

"Well, it's going to sound hard to believe, but our family descends from one of Odin's sons from Asgard. His name was Bragi. Have you ever heard of Bragi?"

I shake my head. I know, from when I looked in the genealogy book, that it stated our family came from Asgard, but I thought that was something that was in every genealogy book, like it was joke, really saying we came from Scandinavia, where Norse mythology originated. Kind of a way of saying we all come from somewhere, just like other families throughout time. I guess that doesn't really make sense. It is certainly possible that Grandpa at least believes that we descend from someone from Asgard. Maybe it's true? I don't really know what to think right now. It's a bit overwhelming.

"Well, Bragi is the second eldest son of Odin, after Thor, and he was born after Odin drank the Mead of Poetry. Normally, Bragi is considered peaceful in the stories and calms people down with his poetry, but over the years, we, as his descendants, have been able to do much more with poetry and sometimes music. We now have the ability to alter decisions and to manipulate elements, to some degree."

I decide to sit down now and try to take some of this in, try to figure out exactly what is happening and what I need to ask Grandpa. I'm still reeling from the sudden change from him mumbling to talking about something pretty far out there.

"Why have I never heard about this before?" I finally ask.

"Well, it doesn't kick in until we turn sixteen, so it wasn't possible for me to know whether or not you would have powers," Grandpa answers. "If you never got them, then I would have to have a different conversation with you. You still would need to know, as you may one day pass it on to your children. I thought I had more time. But, as you can see, time is a fleeting thing."

I shake my head. "So, if you also have these powers, what happened to Grandma? How did you end up in the state you were in for weeks? Why didn't you stop it?"

Honestly, I didn't think about what I said before saying it. Obviously, if he could have done something, he would have. Right?

He drops his head in grief, and I immediately feel terrible for questioning him like that.

"I didn't realize that the people we were talking to were from Loki's line, In fact, we all thought their line was taken care of ages ago." he starts to explain. "I certainly didn't know they had a contraption to extract my essence. All I remember is being cuffed to a table, and after I came to, I couldn't talk because they had gagged me. I had enough essence left to force myself to say that rhyme over and over to myself and hope you or your sister would inherit the powers and say it back to me someday. I never saw what happened to Grandma; is she okay?" He looks around like she may pop up at any moment.

I start to tear up. He doesn't know ...

"Grandpa"—I hesitate—"she was found dead in the kitchen, and you were in the living room with a pile of photos in your lap."

Grandpa stares at me, looking shocked, and then he breaks down in tears.

I do my best to hold him and comfort him, but I don't know what to say. Then again, I don't think there is anything I can say. I need to be here for him and have him here for me, in a deep embrace, letting our emotions out the only way we know how. We cry.

It's a lot for Grandpa to process. The love of his life is gone, and he wasn't even able to say goodbye before she passed. Not to mention, he missed her funeral.

"Do you want to see the program from her funeral and her obituary?" I ask him.

He nods.

I go to find it, and when I come back, as I hand it to him, I tell him, "We had family from all over the country come, including Great-Aunt Phyllis and more cousins than I ever knew existed. We had it here in Grinwell, and tons of friends and neighbors came to the funeral."

"She would have loved that, Jon. Thank you for taking care of all this when I couldn't."

I go on to explain, "You were taken to a lot of different doctors, and they decided you couldn't live alone anymore, so we moved you here with all your stuff and put your house on the market."

He is doing his best to take all this in, but it is a lot to process. I also realize I need to tell him about his car.

"Mom and Dad gave me your Corolla for my sixteenth birthday, but I totally understand if you want it back."

Grandpa chuckles. "I wouldn't dream of it. I'm glad you got the car. I just can't believe everything that they took from me. We have to stop Loki's line from doing this to any of us ever again."

Grandpa shakes his head, tears still in his eyes. "First, let's talk a bit more about your powers. I need to get my mind off your grandmother." He chokes up again before clearing his throat. "What has happened to you since you discovered them? Have you noticed the strange coincidences you talked about earlier?"

Nodding in understanding, I do my best to catch him up to speed on getting the car, the grade in English, and then the snow day. He is particularly interested in the snow day.

"Oh my ... Without any training or special rhymes, you were able to manipulate the weather?"

Looking sheepish, I say, "Well, apparently, there was supposed to be a snow storm, according to the forecast, so I'm not so sure about that."

He smiles, which is nice to see after a rough hour or so of explaining everything that has happened since he was in a daze.

"Does anyone know about what you can do?" he asks in all seriousness.

"Well, Marc knows, and he mentioned something to Jill, but she thinks that both of us are crazy."

Grandpa laughs a little at that one. "I don't really blame her. It is a lot to take in sometimes. I would have rather told you in a different way and gave you more time to adjust to this reality, but we can't always pick our timing. Clearly."

He looks lost in thought again, and then he asks, "So, has anyone new come to town who may seem a bit ... strange or who is causing any kind of trouble?"

"Well, there is a new kid, Dustin, and he kind of likes to bully everyone, even the varsity quarterback! His dad is the wrestling coach, and he was the wrestling state champion last year ... as a freshman."

Grandpa rubs his hand through his large and now unruly beard. "Loki's disgraced and dangerous line is full of wrestlers. In fact, the guy who came to visit me was pretty large and could easily have been a wrestler. He was interested in getting to know us better. I thought he might be a long-lost relative, so I kept talking to him. He took us to a place where he had a collection of Norse artifacts, but one of those artifacts ended up being the device that took my essence. That's the last thing I remember, and I have no idea how Grandma and I got back to the house. I guess he took us home when he was done."

I need to ask him more, so I start with, "How exactly do our powers work for us?"

"It's different for each of us, and our strength also varies, but it is definitely strongest when we are younger. You can say poems to calm people down and even impact them in other ways, but it's important to be careful."

I nod, more than happy to be careful once I understand more about what that means.

"When you say *be careful*, what do you mean?"

"Well, you never know how it is going to impact the person or for how long they will be impacted by what you say. These are powerful suggestions, almost a bit like hypnosis. They may get stuck under your command, and there may be other consequences to what they do under your influence." He pauses then reluctantly asks, "Have you done anything with this gift in public for any reason?"

I immediately drop my head.

"It's okay, Jon. You didn't know what was happening to you. But I need you to tell me what you did."

I might as well start from the beginning. "Well, that new kid, the state champion, has been giving Marc and me a hard time. He wrestled me in gym class the other day and threw me around like I weighed nothing. We accidentally crossed him a couple more times, so he warned us that Marc was going to be his wrestling partner next in gym class." This next part is a bit harder to say, because I don't want him to be disappointed or to get Marc and me in any kind of trouble. "So, before class, I said a poem to give Marc strength and speed, and then the most bizarre thing happened. Marc totally destroyed Dustin, the champ, and threw him around as easily as the champ had thrown me around. It was pretty amazing!"

"What happened after Marc beat him?" Grandpa asks.

"That's the weird thing. Ever since that happened—which was today, by the way—I haven't heard from Marc, like, at all. Apparently, our gym teacher, Coach Locke, took him some place for a snack or something, and I only know that because Mom talked to his mom. He hasn't called or texted me personally yet."

Grandpa is starting to look worried. "This sounds like it could be a problem. It's possible that someone thinks Marc is an Asgardian because of the power he displayed."

I hadn't thought of that before. How exactly is he going to explain his sudden innate ability to wrestle, coupled with his newfound strength?

"Do you think it's possible that Coach Locke and Dustin are Asgardians, too?" I ask.

Grandpa nods slowly. "It's possible ... Do you have a picture of this new coach by chance?"

He was actually in the local newspaper, which we keep old copies of for recycling, so I show him the picture, and he instantly recognizes him.

His jaw drops, and then he says, "That's him, Jon! That's the guy who killed Grandma and took my essence from me."

No More Games

Dustin

COACH AND I HEAD BACK downstairs to resume our interrogation with Marc, and we find that he has been trying to free himself but has succeeded in only marking up his arms and causing his ankles to bleed from the shackles.

"Going somewhere, Thor?" I ask.

He looks up with defeat in his eyes. "No."

When he drops his chin to his chest, I decide that now may be a good time to see if I can get him to talk.

"Did you talk with anyone before gym class today?"

He shakes his head. "Nobody other than Jon. We had lunch together right before gym, as you know, like every other day."

I nod. Indeed, I do know. "What did the two of you talk about?"

Marc thinks for a minute. "We talked about his new car, which used to belong to his grandpa, but now that he is living with Jon, he doesn't need a car anymore."

Coach jumps in and asks, "Why did his grandpa move in with Bragg and his parents?"

"He hasn't been doing well. He is having some issues, and the doctors can't figure out how to help him."

"What kinds of issues?" Coach asks.

"So," I interrupt, wanting to know more about what else was said before gym class, "what else did you and Jon talk about?"

Coach looks at me as he sternly repeats himself, "What kinds of issues is Jon's grandfather having, Miller? Tell me now!"

Marc is a little hesitant but relents. "He's in a wheelchair and having trouble doing anything for himself, probably just because he is old."

"Well, can't his wife take care of him?"

"No, she passed away recently, so it's just his grandpa."

At that moment, I know exactly where this is going. Coach is thinking that Jon's grandpa is the Asgardian that he drained, which would make Jon our special friend. What I don't understand is that I wrestled Jon and felt absolutely nothing. Why was that?

Coach must be having the same issues, because he calls me back upstairs with him for another discussion.

"Are you sure you didn't feel anything from Bragg when you were wrestling him the other day?" he asks.

I shake my head. "You saw what happened to him. So, he is either the world's greatest actor, or he literally has no special strength, speed, or durability. I'm confident that there was nothing magical about him when we wrestled, at least not like I felt with Marc."

"But it sounds like I paid a visit to his grandfather recently," Coach muses. "His grandmother passing away and the grandfather being in a compromised state is too much of a coincidence. We need Miller to talk more about Jon."

I nod, and then we go back down to Marc, who hasn't moved a muscle this time. He has basically accepted the fact that this isn't going to end well for him. It sure didn't take long to break him, but that's also not a great thing. We need him to have some hope.

"Marc, do you want to get out of here?" I ask.

He looks over at me. "More than anything!"

"All you have to do is help us understand what happened. How did you get the strength to beat me at wrestling? You know now that I have special skills that should have made it impossible for you to do what you did, so either you did it yourself or someone helped you. Which is it?"

He looks the other way, and I think Coach and I can both tell that he's trying to not snitch on a friend.

Coach outright asks, "Did Jon give or do something that helped you before you wrestled today?"

"I don't know." Marc is doing everything he can to avoid eye contact.

"Miller," Coach starts yelling, "what did Jon give you or do to you?"

He shakes his head vigorously and says, "No, I will never tell you."

Coach grabs the crown that will go on his head and sets it down just a little but enough to poke into his skull and draw a little blood. Marc screams in pain.

"Tell me what he did, or I will end you right here and now!"

Marc is delirious at this point, sobbing, and then he finally gives in.

"Okay, okay!" He looks down. "I'll tell you."

Still standing over him, Coach says, "You better do it quickly, because I am completely out of patience, Miller!"

He whispers, "He said a rhyme to give me strength and the knowledge to defeat Dustin. He wanted to make sure I didn't get hurt, that's all. It's not his fault. He doesn't know how powerful he is becoming."

Coach stops. "Wait—you knew he has powers?"

"Yes, he has made things happen a few times, so I put it together and realized Jon was making those things happen with his poetry."

"Bragi!" Coach declares.

"That explains the stupid poem in English class," I add. "And why it worked on Mr. Young."

Marc nods to indicate it's true.

Now that we have the answer we are looking for, we realize we actually have to get Jon to come here now. We are also going to have to figure out how to make Marc forget, or we are going to have to end him to keep our identities safe.

Okay, first things first. We need to find Marc's phone so we can send a message to Jon. Bragg doesn't know that we know who he is, so there shouldn't be any real problems. That said, it would be best if he just thought he was coming to meet Marc, or maybe to pick Marc up.

"Where's Marc's cell phone?" I ask Coach. "I know we took it and turned it off, but I have an idea."

GPS

Jon

IT'S MY TURN FOR MY jaw to drop, and now I know where this feeling of dread has been coming from. Marc is in real trouble, and I don't know what I should do about it.

"What should I do?" I ask Grandpa. "What can I even do with these powers? Is there anything that might be able to stop them?"

Grandpa holds up his hand for me to let him talk, so I stop to listen.

"We really don't have enough time to teach you everything you need to know. The best thing to do would be to show you how to protect yourself, and then how to take them by surprise. Fortunately, we know what they are going to attempt to do."

I'm so glad that Grandpa is here and that he knows so much.

Grandpa then teaches me about various protection rhymes that I can use to make it harder for them to penetrate my body. Everything he teaches is mostly about self-defense and making sure that any damage I take will be minimal. I don't think I am going to wow anyone with the ability to lift super heavy objects and hurl them around, so I am going to need to be smart with how I use this gift from Bragi.

Grandpa also explains how I can use rhymes to control another person's body and movements, to at least some extent, sort of like what I did to Marc but in reverse. The rhymes make them slower and less effective, amongst other things. Talk about a crash course!

"Do you think I know enough to protect myself so I can go now and try to find Marc before something terrible happens to him?" I ask. "I'll never forgive myself if he gets hurt because of what I did."

Grandpa holds up a finger. "I have one more thing I need to show you. If things get more out of hand than we want them to, then you can use this blood rhyme. Do you know where my books are?"

I nod my head, and then I lead Grandpa out to the garage where we start digging through all of his book boxes, looking for a special book that he hopes Mom and Dad packed away. Thankfully, we sorted through everything already, so it doesn't take long to find the stack he is looking for.

Suddenly, Grandpa grabs one of the really old books. It's the one that I pointed out to Mom that contains the rhyme that Grandpa was repeating. I remember it has some beautiful but strange poems written on its pages.

Grandpa opens it and says, "This is one, they will never see coming. You are going to need to use the element of surprise to your advantage. It does require you to be in at least some pain, so brace yourself for that. The secret is adding power to your own blood while you still control it to weaponize it."

Grandpa walks me through, step-by-step, on how to manipulate every aspect of my mind, body, and blood for this one specific rhyme to work.

When it seems as if I am as ready as I will ever be, I tell Grandpa, "Thank you!"

He responds in kind. "On the contrary, Jon, thank you! Now go help your friend."

I head out the door with the keys to the Corolla.

Before I get to the car, Grandpa comes out with a small bag and says, "Here, take this. You are going to need these items after it is over. Don't worry about what is in there right now," he says when I start to look inside. "It's just a change of clothes and a page from the book of rhymes."

Giving him a curious look, I jump inside the car, start it up, and as I am pulling out, I realize I have no idea whatsoever where I am going. I decide to start on the main drag to see if I can find any sign of them at any of the restaurants in town. This sounds like it will take a while but, in reality, there are only a dozen places or so where Coach Locke would have taken Marc for a snack and to talk, if that story was actually true.

I check all of them out, driving by slowly enough to look inside the windows, but there is no sign of Coach Locke, Dustin, or Marc.

I am not even a little bit surprised that they are not there. That's when I decide to head over to the school to see if I can get into the principal's office to look for Coach Locke's address on file. Surely if anyone knows where he lives, it would be the school. I don't exactly know where they would keep records on teachers, but I think a reasonable place to start would be Mr. Douglas's office. That's also where the student records are, so I can check Dustin's file, as well.

As soon as I get there, I realize I don't have a key and the building is, of course, locked. I decide to try to open the doors anyway, saying, "For all the doors in the school I see, allow me to enter them without a key." Sure enough, when I check again, the door is unlocked.

I really hope that nobody is here, because it is going to be seriously hard to explain how I got into the school if I get caught walking through a supposedly locked door and find someone staring back at me.

So far so good as I make my way to the main office and start looking for personnel files or student records.

I finally find them and pull Coach Locke's file. Unfortunately, he has no address listed. Weird. Then I grab Dustin's file but, of course, same thing.

I don't understand how the school could allow that. Maybe they have a different set of rules for teachers and their children, or maybe they didn't have a place yet when the files were created. The first assumption seems more possible, as they do get other benefits, like free lunches.

I next run to Coach Locke's office and look around there for a letter, a bill—anything that might indicate where they live. He must have a magazine or something laying around.

Nothing.

This guy just does not want to be found, which is smart if you are a raving lunatic from Loki's line. Based on what I know about Loki, it shouldn't be a surprise at all. He seems to always be getting into some kind of trouble in Norse myths.

Walking back to the Corolla, I start to give up hope, wishing I had a way to track Marc.

I try to find him by his cell phone again, but he must have it off because I can't see his location and any calls I make go straight to voicemail.

As I am looking at my phone, though, I get an idea. I wonder if I can find him this way. I don't remember anything about manipulating a phone from Grandpa's book, but it was a quick skim and, well, I'm not sure they had cell phones to manipulate when those books were being written.

"I know that Marc is scared and alone, but guide me to him through the GPS on my phone." With that, my phone starts to set new coordinates, looking for the best way for me to drive there.

The location that pops up is a bit out of town, but I know I could be running short on time, so I need to go as quickly as possible, assuming Marc is there. Why didn't I think of this sooner? This whole powers thing is going to take a bit to get used to, clearly. This would have saved so much time, though.

I spend the drive over there going over the protection rhymes that I need to say to make sure I have those ready to go before getting out of the car. I also need to use one on Marc as soon as I can get close enough to where they are keeping him. Of course, it is still in the realm of possibilities that he is just hanging out with Dustin and Coach Locke, and that he isn't in any danger at all. However, after what Coach Locke did to my grandpa and grandma, there is no way I am going to give him the benefit of the doubt. I am going to assume that they are up to no good and are both incredibly dangerous.

I actually don't know yet if Dustin is an Asgardian or not, but based upon everything I know about him and heard through the grapevine, it certainly makes sense that he has extra abilities since he is so successful in wrestling, first as a freshman and now as a sophomore.

The Call

Dustin

I POWER ON MARC'S PHONE, and of course he has a pin, so I ask Marc, "What is the pin for your phone?" There's no way I am going to let him use facial recognition to open it then activate some emergency call to the police or something.

He offers it immediately. "It is THOR—8-4-6-7."

"Clever. Ha, what a dork! I bet you regret being so into Thor now, don't you?"

"Not really," he says. "It's not like a descendant of Thor has me locked up in a basement, threatening to kill me or anything."

I know I should be offended by that, but it is a little funny, so I laugh. "I guess that's a good point."

I find Jon Bragg in his phone under the name *"Best Friend."* Cute.

Giving Jon a call, the phone rings a few times, which I think is pretty strange. I would imagine these guys talk all the time and basically sit around, waiting for a word from each other at all times.

He finally picks up and says something like, "Marc, where are you?"

I jump right in with a bright, cheery voice and say, "Oh, hey Jon! This is Dustin Locke. Marc and I have been hanging out ever since he kicked my butt in wrestling. Coach had a few things he wanted to show Marc while we try to recruit him for the wrestling team and, well, Marc thinks you might like to see the artifacts Coach showed him, too."

"Oh, okay, if he thinks so," Jon replies. "Hey, can I talk to Marc?"

JON BRAGG BLUE ESSENCE

I shake my head, even though he can't see me. "Nah, he had to use the bathroom real quick, but he said I could give you a call and invite you over here."

Jon seems agreeable as he says, "Sure, just give me your address, and I'll come over and check it out, plus give Marc a ride home."

"That sounds perfect! The address is 1401 Highway 6. We have a small farmhouse about a mile off the highway. There are two huge trees on either side of our driveway entrance."

"Got it," Jon says. "I'll see you soon!"

I hang up, saying, "Well, that was easier than I thought."

"Yeah, friends do that for each other," Marc says. "They come and get you when you need a ride, and they try to save you when people hold you hostage in a basement and threaten to kill you!"

I shake my head. "We don't want to kill you if we don't have to, Marc. Think about how hard it would be to explain what happened to you with your death all over the news. It would bring too much heat on us, and we don't want that kind of attention. We already have to hear about Mr. Keith's death too often for us to be comfortable."

"Yeah right, Dustin. Like I'm going to believe anything you or Coach Locke say ever again."

I shrug. I really don't care if he believes me or not. I also don't blame him. I certainly wouldn't believe me either. Understandable skepticism, to say the least.

Coach and I spend some time figuring out how to lure Jon down to the basement without having him hear Marc when he inevitably starts screaming.

"Okay, so the first step is to gag Marc so he cannot scream."

Coach agrees. "Yes, that is a good idea."

"Then it's likely that, if we say Marc is downstairs, Jon will unknowingly walk right into our little trap. We can also assume Jon is not experienced with his powers yet, which gives us at least a significant advantage. Of course, he also doesn't have any blue serum to boost his powers with. And whatever the maximum dosage of that is, I think both of us should take before Bragg gets here."

Coach nods.

At least that much is decided.

Coach then says, "We need to be pretty careful with the Bragi line. They are not like the rest, and Loki and Bragi have a feud that goes all the way back to our origins."

"Why do we have to be careful when we are stronger, faster, and more experienced?" I ask.

"Because, like Jon himself, we don't really know yet what he is capable of. We should especially protect our ears from being able to hear him spin his magic with words."

That said, we both jam as much cotton into our ears as we can. While it mutes sounds, it is far from perfect. I suspect that, if Jon speaks even a little louder than normal, I am not going to have any problem hearing him. I think I am going to go with the plan of striking first, fast and hard.

I make my way back to where Marc is and can't resist saying, "You know, you are a really good listener when someone stops you from talking so much."

He screams in anger, undeniably wanting that gag removed, but there is zero chance of that until we have Bragg under our control and are preparing to drain him.

You know what? That screaming isn't going to be okay either.

"Look Marc, if you scream when Jon gets here, I am going to have to kill him before he gets down the stairs, so you better keep quiet if you value your friendship with Jon."

I can tell by the look in his eyes that he understands and is prepared to cooperate.

This is an exhilarating feeling and an opportunity to show Coach how strong I can be. I sure hope Jon puts up a fight. I would really like to see his blood on my hands. I don't want to kill him—I really want his essence—I want to beat him into submission.

I decide to let Marc know, "I am going to really make Jon feel some pain after the two of you embarrassed me today. Honestly, I'm glad it's him so I can have the extra satisfaction of taking yet one more thing from him."

I hear a car pull up the driveway.

Huh, he got here a lot faster than I expected, but that has to be him. Who else would come out into the middle of the country at night?

We hear Jon mess with his keys as he makes his way to the front door. Then we hear three crisp knocks on the door.

Knock. Knock. Knock.

Mom Faints

Jon

DUSTIN TELLING ME THAT Marc was in the bathroom made no sense. I mean, okay, but why would he give him his phone to call me then go to the bathroom? Yeah, that doesn't have any logic to it at all. Then I remember I am dealing with the not-so-clever mind of Dustin.

He wants me to come and meet up with them so they can show me something? Right ... After talking with Grandpa, I have a pretty good idea what it is they want to show me, and I'm not interested in seeing that. However, I just played along on the phone, because one thing is for sure—Dustin may be special, but he does not have super intelligence going for him. At least now I know for certain that Dustin is in on it with Coach Locke, and I can guess that is consistent with him having powers.

Before I get too close and while I am still on the edge of town, I stop at a convenience store and decide to call Grandpa. I'm pretty sure he doesn't have a mobile phone, so I call our home phone and, to my surprise, Mom picks up.

"Jon, you are in luck. We just got home, and I barely got to the phone on time. Where are you? You know it is a school night, right? Not to mention you are supposed to be watching your grandpa."

"Marc needs my help, so I ran out real quick. Can I please talk to Grandpa?"

"Jon, that isn't funny," she says firmly. "You know Grandpa cannot speak with you."

Hearing his name, I guess, Grandpa shouts, "Is that Jon?"

Then I hear the phone fall to the floor before Grandpa picks up and says, "Jon?"

"What just happened?" I ask.

"Well, it appears your mom fainted, but she seems to be okay now. Yep, your dad is helping her up."

"Yeah, I could have probably thought of a better way to tell her you're okay again."

Grandpa laughs. "I don't know. That was kind of fun. What do you need?"

I explain, "I eventually figured out how to use my GPS to take me to where Marc is, but a funny thing happened. Dustin called me and invited me over to see something. I suspect the element of surprise might be gone, Grandpa."

"Yeah, I guess that means they got to Marc, and he told them that you empowered him to defeat Dustin," Grandpa says in a hushed voice. "You need to be careful now, Jon. They are extremely dangerous."

I can hear more movement on the other end of the line. It sounds like Dad and Jill are trying to figure out what is going on and helping Mom.

"Go ahead and take care of what is happening there so everyone can give you a big hug," I tell him. "And Grandpa, if anything happens to me, I love you."

"Jon Bragg," he replies sternly, "you are a Bragi. Nothing is going to happen that you cannot handle. I'll see you soon. And don't forget to look in the bag when this is all over!" With that, he hangs up.

Okay, well, I guess I'm on my own to go after at least two Asgardians who want to extract my essence from me, which sounds unpleasant. I don't really want to lose something that I just found out I have. Who knows what else they are planning?

I pull out of the convenience store parking lot and head toward uncertainty with my stomach twisting in knots and all kinds of negative thoughts swirling around in my head. I am worried that I don't know enough to be able to defeat them both. I also really don't want to do anything that could make things worse for Marc.

I turn off the highway and onto their driveway. It is a gravel one, so I hear every rock spinning under the tires as I approach the house and come to a skidding halt on the rocks, snow, and ice mixture.

Well, there is no turning back now. They definitely heard that noise.

"On this night, and the grounds of this farm, make it so Marc Miller suffers no harm," I quickly say.

That should help protect Marc. Now I need one for me.

"On this night, may my blood run thick and contain enough power for this mystical trick ..."

Okay, well, that is step one. Now I have to find the strength to knock on the door.

When I do knock on the door, Coach immediately opens it up, like he was already waiting on the other side, and says, "Hey, Bragg, we've been watching for your car. Marc and Dustin are downstairs, so you can head on down to hang out with them. I'll be down in a little bit to show you how everything works."

I say, "Thank you, Coach Locke. I can't be too long, though, because Mom just called to remind me it's a school night." Translation: *I am pretty sure I know what you are going to show me, and I have no desire to stick around and see that firsthand.*

I know I should be terrified of this large man, but I am simply furious with him. When I look at him, I can only picture Grandpa stuck in that wheelchair, babbling that rhyme for weeks on end. This monster in front of me did that to him. On top of that, he murdered my grandma.

No, now is not the time. I need to get downstairs before I do something stupid and get Marc to safety. First things first.

As I walk down the stairs and into a creepy basement, which is not as finished as I expected, I hear some movement down there and a muffled voice a bit farther away. Then I am about halfway down the stairs when something reaches out and grabs one of my feet. I immediately trip and tumble down the stairs, and before I know it, there is total darkness as someone hits the lights. I hit my head hard, yet I struggle to get to my feet as quickly as possible.

"Marc? Dustin? Are you guys down here?"

I decide to use my phone as a flashlight and look around for a light switch when the lights suddenly come back on and I see him.

Marc is bound and gagged, tied to a chair, staring at me with sorrow in his eyes.

"Hi, Marc, I see they got tired of listening to you," I tease.

He shakes his head, but I know he is smiling some, because that was pretty funny.

Just then, I get hit from behind, thrown to the floor, and before I know it, I have Dustin on top of me. This is a familiar feeling, unfortunately.

"Hello, Bragg, or should I say, Bragi?"

Great, as expected, he knows.

The Descendants Fight

Dustin

"MAKE IT SO I CAN STAND and give Dustin a hard place to land," Jon says loud enough for me to hear through the cotton plugs, and before I know it, I am thrown back and hit my head against the concrete wall. Then Bragg is on top of me.

"So, should I call you Locke or *Loki*?"

Oh, I see now. He knows about Coach and me, as well.

Well, this indeed should be interesting.

I grin up at him. "I'm glad you know, Bragi. It will make this a much more challenging fight."

I kick him off of me, and he goes flying backward, crashing into the opposite concrete wall with a resounding *thud*. When he walks away from that, I know something is definitely protecting him, because that should have been a knockout blow.

Bragg brushes himself off and forcefully says, "Make this Loki before me freeze and drop him down to his knees."

Suddenly, I have no control over my body whatsoever. I am unable to resist as I drop to my knees, exactly like he said.

I knew that cotton was a stupid idea. I bet Coach knew it, too. That's probably why he isn't down here yet.

What do I do now? I can't move a muscle!

Bragg walks over and starts to talk. "It's not so nice, is it? That's a lot like what your father, Coach, or whatever, did to my grandfather. I have half a mind to leave you like this. You definitely deserve it, or at least your father does."

190

"I didn't have anything to do with that, Bragg," I tell him. "I just found out about all this stuff a few days ago. I didn't even know that I had any advantages in wrestling. Coach completely tricked me."

"But you are undeniably fighting me now." Jon looks down at me with disgust.

I shrug. "It's not like I have much of a choice in the matter. I figured it's you or me."

As I say this, I hear Coach come running down the stairs.

I turn to him and say, "I'm sorry, Coach."

As usual, he ignores me, heading straight for Jon. He starts punching him relentlessly, and even I am quieted as I see him trying to beat the life out of someone.

Bragg is taking a lot of damage, but he somehow still stays conscious and tries to fight back.

Coach has one hand over Jon's mouth the entire time and is beating him ceaselessly with the other, telling him, "I know better than to let you speak! I'm not gonna let you use your powers to get out of this one, Bragi!"

It's in that moment that I realize how stupid I have been. That is the obvious move, and I should have thought of that.

As Jon gets beaten, I start to recover the ability to move a little bit of my body at a time.

Jon, who has received a severe amount of damage, which took a rather long time and a lot of force from Coach, finally passes out.

That's when Coach looks at me and says, "That is how you have to do it with his kind. If you let them talk, they will defeat you. You have to be smarter than that."

I nod, finally having full control over my body again.

"Help me get him on the table," Coach demands. "Once he is there, we can wake him up and carefully ask him some questions."

We put Bragg in the place where Miller once was and use the iron cuffs to lock in his arms and legs. As I am doing that, Coach goes and grabs some blue essence and waves it under Bragg's nose. It only takes a couple sniffs before he wakes up, but before he can say anything, Coach covers his mouth again.

"I'm going to ask you some questions, and I need you to answer them, or I am going to kill your friend over there, and then I am going to kill you and the rest of your entire family. I want you to blink twice for yes and once for no. Do you understand?"

Bragg blinks twice.

"I assume your grandfather is the Asgardian I withdrew essence from after killing his wife a few weeks ago; is that correct?"

Bragg tears up but blinks twice again.

"Do you have any more people in your family who have ascended?"

Bragg blinks once.

Coach clarifies, "So, your father or mother never ascended? Any siblings ascend?"

Bragg again blinks once.

"That's interesting, Bragg. Sorry to hear that. I guess that leaves you with nobody to train you. Well, other than a babbling old man." Coach laughs but pulls up enough for Bragg to bite his hand. Coach reacts by quickly releasing his hand, and then I dive in really quickly with a blow that knocks Bragg back out.

Coach nods. "Nice job, son. You're learning."

Wait—did he just call me *son*. Finally, we have something that has brought us together!

"Thanks, Dad," I reply. "I'm learning from the best."

"Don't get too cocky about it! Do you think you can hold him for a minute? I need to go upstairs and grab some supplies so we can test his essence. I don't think we need to ask him any more questions. At this point, we need to extract what we can and silence the two of them."

I nod. "I got this."

He heads back upstairs, and I relish the fact that we just had a true father/son bonding moment, for probably the first time ever. It wasn't a storybook moment, but it was a moment.

Inside Out

Jon

I START TO COME TO a bit and find I am lying down on something cold. A table? It certainly doesn't feel like the floor, something about how the air moves around me. However, I don't move a muscle, and I don't open my eyes., wanting them to believe I am out cold and not playing possum I need time to think. First, let me assess the situation.

I don't feel anything on my mouth right now, so they haven't gagged me and the restraints seem to be damaged, at least I don't feel the same pressure on my wrists or ankles. Because of that, I am going to assume they think I am passed out completely.

I think I need to get ready for the rest of the blood rhyme that Grandpa taught me from his book of poems. He said to only use it if it was a last resort. Well, I think this qualifies.

I don't feel anything poking into my head or soreness around my skull like Grandpa said he felt, so I am also assuming that they haven't completed or started the extraction yet. I should still be able to use my powers.

I wait patiently now for what Grandpa said they did to him next.

Wait—I hear someone coming down the stairs again. Heavy steps, so I assume it's Coach Locke. Then I hear his footsteps as he crosses the basement and sets something down on the table between my legs. I hear him unzip something then some jostling sounds before he says, "So, I don't have to do this, but I like to test the potency of his essence before attempting the extraction. To do that, we take some of his blood, using the same method a nurse would to collect a blood sample."

I feel Coach tie or slip rubber of some kind around my left arm, and it snaps and pulls a little, which is pretty hard to ignore. I then feel the needle go into my arm. It is a quick prick, but boy, do I hate needles. I resist the urge to squirm, glad that I am not seeing the blood pour into the vials. I have never been able to look at that without getting lightheaded.

After he supposedly fills a couple vials, I feel the needle get removed and some pressure at the site of where the needle was inserted when he bandages it up.

Well, isn't that nice of him to be worried about a little blood after beating the daylights out of me?

Then he says, "To test the blood, we open up a vial and pour the blood into this chalice. I know that sounds gross and, well, it would be if he were human, but because of the Asgardian essence, once in the chalice, it will taste pretty much like the blue serum we drink every week, stronger."

I think to myself, *Wait—they are basically drinking blood every week? Gross.* I will have to mention that to Grandpa later.

I hear them both react pleasantly to the sip of blood, and then Coach Locke says, "See? It's kind of strange, but it tastes fine. That is the way to know for sure that you have an Asgardian. I do recommend, though, that you have a pail handy because, when you are wrong, human blood is absolutely disgusting."

"I'll take your word on that," Dustin says.

"Oh, it will happen to you, too, wait and see." I can hear a hint of humor in Coach Locke's voice.

I can't tell exactly what is going on now, but someone is working around the table. I can hear them, probably Coach Locke, connecting things together and pumping something that sounds a bit like when you are sitting in the barber's chair and they raise your seat up. Speaking of hair, I feel some pressure as something is being slid onto my head.

I think of anything possible to keep myself still, needing just a little more time. I need time for the blood to reach its destination.

As I start to feel the pressure tighten on my head, I know it has to be now. So, without wasting any more time, I start to chant first in my mind,

May my blood that freely flows,
Fuel my power as anger grows,
To end these evil beings from the inside,
And send them on their final ride.

I say it to myself three times, and when I hear them both drop to the floor, I then open my eyes and shout,

"MAY MY BLOOD THAT FREELY FLOWS,
FUEL MY POWER AS ANGER GROWS,
TO END THESE EVIL BEINGS FROM THE INSIDE,
AND SEND THEM ON THEIR FINAL RIDE!"

They gasp for breath and writhe in obvious pain as my blood tears through them.

Meanwhile, I break free and run over to Marc and remove his gag then untie him from the chair that he was bound to for who knows how long.

We are both moving as quickly as we can as I say to him, "What do you say we get the heck out of here?"

He beams at me. "I thought you'd never ask!"

As I walk past Coach Locke and see the pain he is going through, I tell him, "My grandpa said to say hello and to tell you that this is for his wife. Goodbye, Coach Locke—I mean, Loki!"

With that, I turn to Marc and say, "Let's get out of here. This place is going to get really messy, really fast!"

As we run up the stairs and out the door, we hear a scream, and then another, each followed by the loudest popping noises I have ever heard. It leaves a sickening feeling in my stomach.

I didn't want to have to do that, but they left me with no choice.

That blood rhyme can only be used after someone has consumed your blood. It causes the blood to race through the whole body, expand, and it literally explodes through the skin as it escapes the person who consumed it. It sounds awful in every way, and if Coach Locke hadn't consumed some of Grandpa's blood before extracting his essence, we would not have known to expect it. So, this is a case where his past actions led to his demise in a literal way. Through this, Grandpa got his revenge and, just as importantly, we keep other Asgardians safe.

As we get into the Corolla, Marc stares at me. I can only imagine how terrible this whole thing was for him. It was terrible for me, and I knew it was coming. Plus, I have the special ability to deal with it. But Marc just had to suffer, and all because I gave him the ability to beat Dustin in a stupid wrestling match. He also saw me do something so terrible that we will both never be able to forget it. I don't know if he will ever forgive me or look at me the same.

I really don't know what to say to him, so I decide to go with, "I'm sorry. I'm sorry you had to go through all that pain tonight, and I'm sorry you had to see me do that to them."

His eyes get big, and he now has the biggest smile on his face as he says, "THAT. WAS. AWESOME!"

Better Days

Jon

BEFORE WE HEAD HOME, Marc tells me about everything that happened to him since gym class. Coach Locke and Dustin really did a great job of tricking him by using his love of Thor to lure him to their place. I can't believe they took that long to connect him to their machine, though.

Oh wait! I need to look in the bag that Grandpa packed for me.

As I look inside, I see a change of clothes for each of us and a poem from the book that looks to be for healing.

I read the poem aloud,

"Repair our bodies,
Of all cuts and bruises,
As we leave this deadly site.
Make it so there is no evidence,
That we have been in,
And won the fight."

With that, I stare in awe as Marc's skin starts to heal, and then I turn to look in the rearview mirror when I feel my skin stitching up.

Wow! This is crazy.

We then quickly swap out of our stained clothes and into the clean ones that Grandpa sent, now looking as if nothing happened.

That reminds me, we also need to get our hands on that extraction device so we can destroy it. The last thing we need is for some other warped Asgardian to find out what it is used for then start hunting us down again. The world would be a much better place if that machine was destroyed. At least for all of us out there holding onto our blue essence.

That said, I have no desire to go back into that house where I actually ended the lives of two people. I know they were threatening my best friend, my family, and me, but I don't yet know how to process the fact that I actually killed them, and in such a brutal, vengeful way at that. No, I need to just stay away from there for a good, long while. Maybe forever.

As I pull up to Marc's house, he is still going on about being my sidekick. Honestly, I'm just glad to hear his voice and that he's safe. The fear of almost losing him really made me appreciate my best friend that much more. In addition, he was actually right—not that we can rub it in Jill's face—but Marc knew me so well that he was able to tell when I was manipulating things with my poems to get what I want. I think that says something about our relationship. I'm really lucky to have a friend like that, and I think he feels the same.

I decide to tell him, "Marc, thank you for being a good friend and for believing in me when I didn't believe in myself."

"You're welcome. But that's what best friends and sidekicks are for!"

We both laugh, and then I wave at him as he heads inside his home, safe and sound and back in civilization. Well, at least as we know it.

As soon as I pull into the driveway, back at home, I see Grandpa outside waiting for me. And, as I get out of the Corolla, he walks up and asks, "Well, how did it go?"

"It went exactly as we thought it would," I tell him. "The important thing is Marc and I got home safely and they will never bother anyone ever again."

As I finish this sentence, Mom comes out and says, "Get back in here, Dad. I don't want you to push yourself too hard, too quickly."

He pats me on the back and shouts out, "Good, good deal. I'm glad the Corolla is treating you well, Jon."

I look at him and grin. "It sure is, Grandpa. Thank you!" I then walk over to Mom.

"When did Grandpa start talking to you?" Mom asks.

"I am not completely sure ... Sometime after you left earlier." I shrug. "It really surprised me when he said my name, that's for sure. It was a great feeling!"

"Yes, we are all really glad," Mom says. "What did Grandpa and you talk about?"

"Didn't Grandpa tell you?" I ask.

"No, he just said it was something between the two of you."

I nod and agree. "Yes, that definitely is true. Almost everything he said was just for the two of us. He's amazing, Mom!"

Mom nods in agreement and says, "That he is, Jon-boy, that he is."

"I am a Bragi after all!" Grandpa says, having heard us talk.

Mom and I exchange knowing smiles and walk inside, following in Grandpa's footsteps.

Once I get inside, I join the conversation that seems to have been going on when I pulled up as everyone catches Grandpa up on all the things he missed over the last several weeks. It is so great to see him talking again, even though I know how much his heart is aching from losing Grandma. We are talking about having a small service so he can say his goodbye to her properly like the rest of us had the chance to do. We don't want him to have to go through that alone.

One by one, we all eventually head to bed for the night, with Grandpa and I going last, as if nothing major happened over the last few days, like finding out I have magical powers and am a descendant of Bragi. Which reminds me, I need to research Bragi to understand what he did over time, other than calm people down with his poetry. I have never heard of him before now. I knew of Odin, Thor, and Loki, but not Bragi. Of course, Grandpa can help me out with all that and then some, especially now that we are roommates.

After the battle tonight, it's a good feeling to know I can defend myself, but I am starting to understand why Grandpa told me earlier that I need to be careful. Clearly, this power we have isn't something to play around with or treat lightly.

Before going to sleep, I have a chance to talk with Grandpa about what happened now that we are alone.

I start by saying, "They tried to attack me right away, as we talked about. They definitely knew I had powers before I got there. Coach Locke sent me to the basement, and Dustin tripped me going down the stairs."

Grandpa isn't surprised.

"How quickly did they try to gag you?" he asks.

"Dustin took a bit of punishment before Coach Locke came down, covered my mouth, and beat me until I passed out."

Grandpa shakes his head. "I'm sorry, Jon."

"You know what? We don't need to rehash this. It's not important. We fought, and I eventually won. But what I think is important is that we get their equipment and destroy it before anyone figures out what it can be used for."

Grandpa agrees, but then he pauses for a bit, and I can tell he's trying to decide whether or not to say something.

"What, Grandpa?" I prompt him. "You can tell me anything now."

He grins. "I suppose so." He carefully begins, "There is a secret group called the Asgardian Protection Society, whose job is to make sure that the descendants of Asgard neither abuse their powers nor accidentally become discovered. Ages ago, this is the group that punished Loki's line for violating nearly every rule generation after generation. They had to be stopped. So their essence was put out, or so we thought. Apparently, they found a loophole. I only know about all of this as I used to be an active member of this group when I was younger. I have a few contacts that might be able to help us out with this little problem. We really don't want the wrong people to find the

Lockes or their equipment. I'll make some calls and see how quickly it can be done.

"As you have ascended, I will need to register you with them, anyway, so you can also fall under their protection, for better or worse. It's something that is mandatory, a responsibility passed down from generation to generation, much like our abilities. I'll cover the rules with you over the next few weeks. There aren't too many, but they are sacred to us."

On that note and with the hope of this problem completely going away, I settle in bed and begin writing in my poetry journal about how thankful I am to be lying in a warm, safe place and not on that Medieval table any more where I could have lost everything.

That was such a close call. I'm sure I will be having nightmares for years to come over that little episode. I hope I never feel that vulnerable ever again.

Then, to my surprise, in a matter of minutes, I drift off easily and blissfully into a deep sleep. Probably because Marc is safe, I am a safe, and Grandpa can talk again. Plus, without a doubt, I was completely exhausted, both mentally and physically.

I WAKE UP WHEN MY ALARM goes off and feel a huge weight has been lifted off of me. For the first time ever, I don't have to worry about being bullied in school by anyone. Not because they won't try to make fun of me, but because I am confident in who I am and who I am becoming. I'm sure there will be people who will still tease me for being a book nerd, but I am okay with that. It's clear that my love of poetry and books is going to come in handy time and again throughout my entire life as I learn what it means to be Bragi.

By the time Jill and I get downstairs for breakfast, Grandpa has cooked his special pancakes for us, to thank us all for taking care of him. It's a great way to start the day. Then Jill and I fall back into our comfortable routine of grabbing our gear and getting back into the Corolla to head to school.

I stop by to pick up Marc on the way, and when he jumps in, I say, "Hey, Marc, are you ready for some better days?"

He cocks his head to the side. "Jon, did you see the news this morning on social media?"

"No."

"Apparently, Coach Locke and Dustin have disappeared. Principal Douglas went over to the house they're renting this morning to talk to Coach Locke about bailing out on work yesterday, and it was completely bare. There wasn't a single item of furniture left, and the entire place was spotless."

"What? How is that possible?" I ask.

"I guess we will have to wait and see about those better days."

I shrug. "I guess so."

Of course, I have a pretty good idea that it was the work of the Asgardian Protection Society, which I don't know enough about yet to introduce to Marc. I can only assume that Grandpa was able to reach out to them after all.

I wonder if, someday, I will be asked to be a part of their group like Grandpa. I sure would like to know more about them. Maybe I will find out more as I finish up my genealogy badge and explore our family history. I have so much to learn from Grandpa about these powers, and I would love to trace our line all the way back to Bragi. For now, I will keep it all a secret, scout's honor.

KENNEY MYERS

Thank you for reading:
Jon Bragg
Blue Essence
Watch for more books in the Jon Bragg series here:
Website: https://www.kenneymyers.com[1]
Special Thanks
Kristin Campbell - Editor
Nicole Mullaney - Advisor
About the Author

Kenney Myers is a husband and father of three children living and working in the Houston, TX area. He is originally from a small town in Iowa where he and his wife Jolene were high school sweethearts. You may be familiar with him as an actor in various films and TV shows or as a technology entrepreneur. He is best known for the TV show Kindly Kenney which is distributed worldwide by UKW Media.
You can follow his adventures here:
https://www.imdb.me/kenneymyers[2]
FaceBook, Twitter, & Instagram: @KenneyMyers

---

1. http://www.kenneymyers.com/

2. http://www.imdb.me/kenneymyers

Don't miss out!

Visit the website below and you can sign up to receive emails whenever Kenney Myers publishes a new book. There's no charge and no obligation.

https://books2read.com/r/B-A-KKJN-PZULB

BOOKS 2 READ

Connecting independent readers to independent writers.

www.ingramcontent.com/pod-product-compliance
Lightning Source LLC
Chambersburg PA
CBHW032122170626
46808CB00006B/2067